## "Why are you working here at my hotel?"

"A girl has to earn a living somehow," Charlotte replied, aware of Harris Jordan's stony face.

"So what's it going to take to send you crawling back to the rock you came out from under?" he asked.

She was taken aback by his venom. "What did you say?" she exclaimed.

"You heard me. Don't play dumb. I caught on to that act years ago and you haven't improved on it. I want to know what I have to do to get you out of my life this time."

Furious, she swung around in her chair to face him. "You conceited oaf! You tore through my life like a hurricane leaving nothing but chaos behind. And you know full well you never did want to marry me!"

**SANDRA K. RHOADES** began reading romance novels for relaxation when she was studying for her engineering degree and became completely hooked. She was amazed at how much fun the books are, and before long, her sights were set on a career in romance writing. Colorado-born, she now lives in British Columbia with her husband and their two children. There she raises livestock, and every summer keeps a large garden.

## Books by Sandra K. Rhoades

Don't miss any of our special offers. Write to us at the following address for information on our newest releases.

Harlequin Reader Service
P.O. Box 1397, Buffalo, NY 14240
Canadian address: P.O. Box 603,
Fort Erie, Ont. L2A 5X3

# SANDRA K. RHOADES

## stormy reunion

*Harlequin Books*

TORONTO • NEW YORK • LONDON
AMSTERDAM • PARIS • SYDNEY • HAMBURG
STOCKHOLM • ATHENS • TOKYO • MILAN

To Chris
With love and thanks
for all your support and encouragement

Harlequin Presents first edition July 1991
ISBN 0-373-11381-1

Original hardcover edition published in 1990
by Mills & Boon Limited

STORMY REUNION

# CHAPTER ONE

CHARLOTTE felt the familiar involuntary tightening of her stomach muscles as she entered the dimly lit lounge. Having worked as a cocktail waitress at the Black Stallion Tavern in the Foothills Hotel for nearly a year, she would have thought she'd have grown immune to the vague embarrassment that always assailed her when she first walked in wearing the scanty costume the management called a uniform. However, for the first few minutes she was always acutely conscious of the speclative looks the male patrons treatcd her to as they eyed the cleavage revealed by the low-cut necklinc of her strapless dress, and the long length of her legs below its almost non-existent skirt.

She let nothing of her feelings show, though, as she walked through the room, automatically flashing smilcs at the various customers seated around the tables. Gaining the bar, she rested one foot on the brass rail that fronted it and waved a greeting to the bartender. He came over to her, his eyebrows lifting quizzically as he commented, 'You're in a good mood tonight. What gives?'

'Nothing special.' Charlotte shrugged. 'I was just thinking about quitting, that's all. That always cheers me up.'

'Oh, come on, Charlie. You mean you're not going to miss me in September?' Tony admonished, his mouth pursed in mock chagrin. Unrepentant, Charlotte shook her head and he winced exaggeratedly. 'Next fall, when you're faced with a classroom filled with screaming brats, you're going to regret giving up all this!' His arm swept out in an arc, encompassing the room.

Charlotte had turned aside to retrieve a tray in preparation for the night's work and was grinning when she turned back. 'That'll be the day! It's only the thought of those "brats" that has made me stick it out here all this time. I'd have gotten a decent day-job a long time ago if it hadn't been for them.'

Her smile lingered. It was a source of great pride and satisfaction to her that she had finally earned her bachelor's degree in education, even though it had taken five and a half years instead of the normal four. It had been a long haul, what with working full time, first as a dishwasher until eventually she had got a job as a cocktail waitress where the pay was better.

The struggle was going to be worth it, though. In the autumn she would take on her first class, grade one at a local elementary school. Ever since she was a child she'd wanted to be a teacher, and she knew she was going to love it. Besides, she wouldn't have to work in tight dresses and spike heels!

When Charlotte looked back at her co-worker, he was studying her with a devilish gleam in his eyes. He gestured towards the painting hanging over the back of the bar. 'Since you're set on turning into a staid old schoolmarm. . .why don't you leave us something to remember you by? Now that this place has changed hands, the new owner might let me paint a new picture

for up there.' His grin was wolfish. 'You could pose for
it.'

She tossed him and the oil a derisive glance. It really
was an awful painting. The nude figure draped over a
Victorian love-seat bordered on the obscene. The
woman's breasts were enormous and totally out of
proportion to the rest of her body; her 'seductive' smile
was more of a leer, the 'come-hither' look in her eyes
salacious. Tony undoubtedly would be able to produce
something far more appealing—but not using her as a
model!

'Don't be cute, Tony!'

He gave her a considering look. 'Actually, I'm
serious.'

'Sure you are,' Charlotte mocked. 'And what would
Ann—you remember her, your *wife*—have to say
about my stripping off for you?'

'As a matter of fact, we were talking about it one
day. She thought it was a great idea.'

Charlotte's brows shot up doubtfully, then she
revised her look. Ann probably wouldn't mind. She
was one of the most secure people Charlotte had ever
met. When she and Tony had first developed a friendship, Charlotte had been somewhat worried as to how
his wife would react to her. She wasn't in the least
conceited, but she couldn't help but know that she was
well above average in looks. Long silvery blonde hair,
wide, violet-hued eyes, and a body that curved in all
the right places: Charlotte simply didn't look like the
kind of girl most wives wanted their husbands to be
pals with.

But she and Tony were pals—nothing more—and fortunately Ann understood that.

However, even if Ann didn't mind her posing for Tony in the nude, Charlotte definitely did! 'Well, it's not on, and I don't care what Ann thinks of the idea!' At Tony's look of protest, she quickly changed the subject. 'So when's the new owner taking over?'

'Shame on you.' Tony looked at her with feigned horror. 'You mean you didn't go to the employees' meeting today? Tut, tut, what kind of loyal worker are you? The new boss was there to fill all us peons in on what's going on.'

'You know I wasn't there. So what did he say— what's he like?'

Tony shrugged. 'How would I know? I didn't go either!'

'And you criticise me?' She looked heavenwards.

'We didn't have to go,' Tony assured her. 'I don't know if you had a chance to look at the schedule for tonight or not, but we're working with Linda. She'll fill us in on all the gory details.'

'Too true,' Charlotte said drily. 'Hurry up and get my float: maybe I can be out working the tables by the time she gets here.'

Tapping her foot impatiently, she watched Tony go to the cash register and take out the money she would need to make change. It probably was a little mean of her to want to avoid Linda, but Charlotte wasn't in the mood tonight to listen to one of Linda's long-winded accounts of the happenings at the Foothills Hotel Complex. The girl was unbelievable—for one thing, she actually loved being a cocktail waitress! Before transferring into the lounge a couple of months ago, she'd worked in the coffee-shop, and she considered the change a promotion. She thought the pseudo-dance-hall-girl costumes they wore were 'bad', was flattered when a customer made a pass at her, and had thought it exciting when once a fight had broken out between a couple of patrons who'd had too much to drink. Her exuberant enthusiasm might have been kind of cute, if only she hadn't teamed it with being the biggest gossip in the entire establishment.

Charlotte wasn't going to be able to avoid her tonight, either. She bubbled up to the bar just as Tony was handing over the float money. After offering the younger girl a brief 'hello', Charlotte made a big show of counting her notes, enumerating aloud in hopes of cutting off any attempts by Linda to strike up a conversation. Unfortunately, it didn't work.

'I didn't see you at the meeting this afternoon. I saved a seat for you.'

'I was too busy to come,' Charlotte muttered. 'Fifteen, sixteen. . .'

'You should have made an effort. Boy, did you ever miss out!' Linda informed her with relish.

'Sixteen. . .' Charlotte hesitated. Hadn't she said that already? Scowling down at the stack of notes in her hand, she turned them over to restart the count. She was up to 'three' when Linda's fidgeting convinced her that she might as well hear the girl out, because she would never get the float counted accurately otherwise.

'OK, so what did I miss? Are there going to be a lot of changes?'

'Oh, there was a lot of talk about that stuff, but just seeing the new owner was worth going to the meeting for.' Linda rolled dreamy eyes upwards. 'What a hunk! He's got A.M. like you wouldn't believe.' At her audience's uncomprehending looks she supplied, 'Animal magnetism.'

Tony and Charlotte exchanged glances. Linda must really have been bowled over by the new owner to have missed out on the other details of the meeting. Usually she gave them such a detailed account that they had to wonder if she hadn't taken down the minutes.

She waxed on, 'He is *so* sexy. . .it simply oozes out of him. I bet he could be a movie star if he wanted to. Murray said that he's filthy rich as well. He's going to be living in the penthouse all summer. I wonder if I can get him to notice me,' she questioned speculatively.

Of one mind, Tony and Charlotte turned simultaneously and walked away in different directions. Linda scandalmongering was bad; Linda being starstruck was positively nauseating. While she usually made a play for every halfway-decent-looking guy that walked into the place, Charlotte had never seen her in such a tailspin. For a second, Charlotte felt a twinge of pity for the younger girl. She'd known a fantastic-looking guy once who'd bowled her over with his 'animal magnetism'. It had taught her a harsh lesson that she was unlikely ever to forget!

By the time she returned to the bar with her drink orders, the lounge was filling up with people and there was no time for further conversation. Someone started the jukebox and the nasal twang of a country and western singer competed with the laughter and talk of the customers. It was a Friday night and the locals were out celebrating the end of the working week, competing for space with the hotel guests. As the noise-level rose, Charlotte became wholly occupied with keeping her orders straight as she delivered her drinks.

As she stood at the bar a couple of hours later waiting for Tony to mix the drinks she'd asked for, Charlotte eased her foot out of one sandal and rubbed the arch against the shin of her leg. 'I hate it when we're so busy,' she commented randomly. 'My feet are killing me.'

'Yeah, but how about tips?' Tony reminded her as he placed the filled glasses on her tray. 'No customers, no tips.'

'That's true,' Charlotte admitted, reaching down to replace her shoe. Upright once again, she picked up her tray and prepared to move off. Before she could, though, Tony called out to her.

'By the way, you'd better look extra sharp. I just saw Clark come in with a party and sit down at one of your tables. As far as I know, he's still the manager, so you had better hustle on over there.'

'Well, at least he usually tips well.' Charlotte sighed, not really wanting any more customers—not even big tippers.

Tony winked at her. 'Maybe the guy with him is the new owner. That could be better than a tip, if Linda's description of him is anything to go by. Just be careful all that "A.M." doesn't do you in.'

'Oh, I'm always careful,' she assured him with a grin, glancing over to the far corner of the lounge. Cigarette smoke hung over the tables, creating a haze that made it difficult to make out who was sitting there. However, even in the gloom she could make out Mr Clark's shiny bald pate. There were two women with him as well as a man, though she couldn't make out their features. If the man was the new owner, Charlotte guessed that his famous sex appeal didn't ooze that far in the dark.

Dismissing the matter from her mind, Charlotte moved out into the lounge. 'That will be four eighty,' she said a few minutes later as she set drinks in front of two men. As she waited for one of them to pay her, she mentally ran through the list of drinks she'd have to take out on her next round. Had that one lady really ordered tequila and Coke? It sounded ghastly.

'I'll get this one, Jake,' one of the pair offered, fumbling in his pocket for his wallet and easing himself closer to Charlotte as he did so. His shoulder brushed her thigh, and he grinned up at her with yellowed teeth as she stepped away from him. Keeping his eyes riveted to her cleavage, he extracted a note from the wallet.

Charlotte ignored the leer and reached out to take the bill from him. She had to lean over slightly to reach it and the man seized the opportunity to shove the note into the valley of her breasts, his rough fingers rasping against her smooth skin.

'You can keep the change, honey,' he offered salaciously as Charlotte jumped back and away from his touch. His partner, Jake, sniggered.

Her lips clamped in a tight, furious line, Charlotte pulled the crumpled note from her cleavage and smoothed it out. Five dollars—her mouth tightened further as she glared at the two men. It was bad enough

waiting on lechers, but *cheap* lechers were even worse.
Taking two dimes from the change littering her tray,
she tossed them on the table between the two men.
'Thanks all the same, but I don't accept tips from
creeps.'

The look on their faces was actually kind of funny.
It made one wonder what went on in some people's
heads. Did those two old perverts actually think that
she *liked* being mauled?

Treating them to a final look of contempt, Charlotte
turned to walk away. Unfortunately, Jake's buddy had
already got back on form and retaliated for her barb
by running his hand up the back of her leg to pat her
bottom as soon as her back was turned.

Startled, the empty glasses on her tray rattling, she
swung back around. Furious angry colour stained her
cheeks as she shot a killing look at her molester. She
was a hair's breadth from beaning him with her tray
when she realised that everyone seated at the adjoining
tables was watching the scene with interest. It would
probably cost her her job if she followed through her
inclination. Mr Clark put a lot of emphasis on the
'customer is always right' adage, and he would have a
front-row seat if she gave free rein to her temper.

Choking back her rage, Charlotte turned once again
and stalked away from the two men. With a great deal
of effort, she pulled herself together as she crossed the
few feet of floor to where the manager was seated with
his party and managed a smile for them.

'Good evening,' she greeted the table generally, but
kept her attention focused on her boss. She could be in
big trouble if he had heard her call those two deviants

'creeps', even if they had deserved it. 'What can I get for you?'

The older man gave her a searching look. 'Problems, Charlie?' He nodded his head in the direction of the table she had just left.

'Nothing out of the ordinary, sir. I handled it,' Charlotte assured him.

'Well, that's good. We want to keep our customers happy.'

'Yes, sir,' Charlotte muttered. She wondered how he would feel if he were expected to parade around half naked and let a bunch of strangers paw him. He might not think his customers deserved to be quite so happy then!

Discretion being the latter part of valour, though, Charlotte turned her attention to the older woman at the table and asked for her order. When she'd written it down, Charlotte moved on to the other woman—no, girl, she thought, her heart sinking. She shot Mr Clark a resentful glance, wondering if he was putting her to some kind of test or something. She had worked long enough in bars to spot someone under-age instinctively. If this child was of drinking age, then Charlotte would quit this stupid job and go and apply for her pension!

Mr Clark seemed to be expecting her to take the child's order, though, so Charlotte went ahead and wrote it down. A pink squirrel—that was a kid's kind of drink. Sweet and fruity, it tasted like a milkshake even if it was loaded with alcohol. If the girl wanted to pass for over twenty-one, one would have thought she would at least make an effort to appear older. She wasn't even dressed for the part. Her dark hair was pulled back with a couple of slides from a face devoid of make-up. The dress she wore was pale pink with white lace edging on the high collar and cuffs. She looked as if she were on her way to Sunday school!

Unhappily, Charlotte rejected the idea of asking to see some identification from the girl. Mr Clark probably wouldn't consider that 'keeping the customer happy'. But if the liquor inspector came in and found an under-age girl drinking, Charlotte had no doubt as to who would be the one in trouble. It would be *her* for serving the child in the first place.

Pondering how she was going to handle the situation, she distractedly turned her attention to the other man at the table. At first glance, she decided that he must be the new owner. He certainly lived up to Linda's enthusiastic description, as he was undeniably good-looking in a very sexy, masculine way. His forehead was broad, pleated at the moment in a slight frown, his cheekbones high, his jaw firm and ruggedly cut. As her eyes touched his and she saw the hard glitter of their silvery grey, a jolt of shock went through her as she realised they were not the eyes of a stranger.

Even after all these years, the sight of him sent a sharp pang of joy darting through her. Greedily, she studied his features, marking changes, wondering how she could possibly not have recognised him in that first instant. Of course, it had been six years. Harris had matured from the callow twenty-three-year-old she'd known then: his face was harder, etched with lines of experience; his body had filled out in broad, masculine lines. Nevertheless, he was achingly familiar—the man she had been going to marry, the man whose child she had carried.

Flushed with delight, she moistened her lips to speak his name, but as though anticipating her he interposed suddenly, 'I'll have a Scotch and water.' He looked over to Mr Clark. 'What will you have, James?'

'Make it the same.'

Bewildered, Charlotte watched as the group turned inward, excluding her as they dismissed her. She stood staring at Harris's profile, the sharp thrust of his jaw, the strong line of his nose. Could it be that he hadn't recognised her, didn't remember her? She knew the answer to that. He had. When his eyes had met hers, she'd read the awareness in them.

'Are you going to get our order, Charlie?' Mr Clark reprimanded her sharply.

'Oh, yes, of course.' She struggled out of her daze. She turned and, for one brief instant her gaze locked with Harris's. Yes, he recognised her. His eyes were filled with memories—and bitterness and anger. Quickly, she turned away, hiding her own eyes so he wouldn't see the pain in them.

Charlotte was preoccupied as she waited for Tony to fill her order for drinks. She had often wondered what Harris's reaction would be if they ever encountered one another again. Somehow she hadn't expected him to pretend they were strangers. Maybe it was unreasonable to feel hurt by it, given the way things had turned out with their engagement, but she did none the less. After all, the decision to call off the wedding had been a mutual one.

At least, she thought it had been mutual. They hadn't actually discussed it at the time, but then, what had there been to discuss? The only reason Harris had been going to marry her was because she was pregnant. No baby, no wedding, it had been as simple as that.

Funny that even after all these years it still hurt to think about those weeks of her affair with Harris. Not that they hadn't been joyous times. Looking back, Charlotte sometimes thought they might have been the happiest days of her life. But they had only been a couple of immature kids, playing at the game of love. When reality had caught up with them and it hadn't been a game any more, the good times had ended with a bang.

They had met at the Denver stock show. Charlotte's father was a small-time rancher with big ideas who had brought his cattle to the major show. Charlotte had hated those cows! Maybe things would have been different had her mother been still alive, but she'd died when Charlotte was a toddler. As Charlotte had grown up, it had seemed to her that the only interest in her father's life was his cattle. He had lavished all his time, money and even affection on his bovines. By the time she was seventeen, she'd grown to resent both his animals and him.

She hadn't wanted to go to the stock show with him. It had meant missing school, which she'd loved, and being around his cows, which she hadn't. He'd insisted, though. Consequently she had been in a sulky, rebellious mood when he had dragged her off to meet some big hotel magnate to whom he was hoping to sell some beef. As it turned out, Harris's father hadn't bought the beef, but Charlotte had had an affair with his son.

Her initial overtures to the tycoon's son had been motivated mainly by spite. Her father had been impotent as he'd watched her flirtations, unable to offend a potential buyer. It had given Charlotte silent satisfaction to observe his discomfort as she smiled and talked with the hotelier's handsome son. Despite his obsession with cattle, her father had been a strict parent. He'd never afforded her much freedom and his careful vetting of her potential boyfriends turned most of them off.

It was hard to say when exactly she had stopped seeing Harris as merely a weapon to use against her father, and had become drawn to him as a person on his own account. It wasn't that first night, but it wasn't long afterwards that she had found herself falling headlong in love with him. Even knowing that he only saw her as a light-hearted flirtation, a good companion with whom he could enjoy the carnival atmosphere of the stock show, hadn't slowed that foolish dive into love. She had been young and starry-eyed and obsessed by a man for the first time in her life.

Charlotte bit her lip as she recalled just how obsessed she had been. Harris had been twenty-three, something of a playboy, still sowing his wild oats. Still, he probably wouldn't have taken a seventeen-year-old virgin to his bed, if she hadn't practically dragged him there. As the end of the stock show grew near, Charlotte had grown desperate with fear that it would signal the end of her relationship with Harris. Like so many other rash teenage girls, she had sought to hold him with that most primitive of chains, sex.

Afterwards, she didn't think she had intended to get pregnant that night, consciously planned to use that to force him into marriage. It was only after that scenario had worked itself out that she had begun to wonder if it hadn't been in the back of her mind all along. She loved Harris, would have done just about anything to hold on to him—maybe she *had* gone that far? She just didn't know, and all through their short engagement she had lived with the guilt that maybe she had engineered the unhappy situation.

'What kind of aftershave was he wearing?'

For a brief moment Charlotte stared blankly at Tony. His grin split his face beneath the full moustache he sported as his blue eyes gleamed with devilry. 'What did you say?' Charlotte asked frowningly.

'I asked about his aftershave. If what's he's got is something that comes in a bottle, I'd like to know about it. It could do wonders for my marriage.'

'What who's got?' Charlotte asked peevishly, automatically checking over the tray of drinks on the counter in front of her to see whether Tony had filled her orders correctly. As if she didn't have enough on her mind with Harris's unexpected appearance, without having to put up with Tony's silly riddles.

'The new boss, of course. You're even worse than Linda.'

Charlotte was only half listening to him. The sight of the frothy pink drink on her tray reminded her of the girl sitting with Harris at the Clarks' table. The *child*

must be Harris's companion. Without her being aware
of it, her mouth tightened. She'd been under-age when
they had been dating and he had never taken *her* into
a bar, although she remembered asking him once. It
had bothered her that she was so much younger than
him, banned by law from doing all the 'adult' things an
older woman could. Despite his somewhat wild reputation, though, Harris hadn't been willing to assist her
in circumventing the rules.

'Charlie, the bar's on fire,' Tony said softly.

She didn't even hear him. Now that Harris was
older, apparently his scruples had undergone a change.
However, she wasn't going to let him get away with
bringing some pubescent popsie in here and expecting
her to wait on them!

Snatching up her loaded tray, Charlotte stalked away
from the bar, unaware of Tony's speculative gaze
following her. By the time she reached the Clarks'
table she was seething with resentment. As she set a
whisky sour in front of Mrs Clark, her hand trembled
slightly and a bead of liquid coursed down the side of
the glass. Although she should have served the girl
next, she quickly placed the men's drinks in front of
them instead.

Charlotte hesitated briefly, entertaining sudden
qualms about the advisability of her plan. After all, the
lounge was dimly lit and perhaps she was mistaken
about the girl's age. She gave her a long, assessing look
from behind the veil of her lashes. She was leaning
towards Harris, her kewpie-doll face turned up to his
as he smiled down into her vacuous eyes. She didn't

look a day over sixteen. Harris should be ashamed of himself, the dirty old man!

Charlotte moved around the table towards the girl, stumbling slightly as she reached her. The last drink on her tray slid across it to the edge, and the glass tipped on to its side. The rose-coloured liquid cascaded down into the young girl's lap.

Exploding with a curse that was doubly shocking coming out of the mouth of one so young, the girl shot out of her chair as the icy drink soaked the material of her dress. Outraged, she rounded on Charlotte. 'You stupid, incompetent. . .you moron! How could you be so clumsy?'

'Oh, I'm terribly sorry,' Charlotte offered hastily. She wasn't being sarcastic, either. She'd had no idea the girl would react so violently. It had just seemed like such a good way of getting her out of the Black Stallion without having to serve her.

'Well, you ought to be sorry, you idiot,' the other girl scathed, dabbing at the stain on her skirt and muttering curses under her breath. 'I don't know how they could let anyone so bumbling work here. You should be *fired*!'

'I. . .I don't know what to say. I really am truly sorry,' Charlotte choked, taking up a napkin and reaching over to help the girl clean off her dress. She had her hand slapped for her pains and, biting her lip, stood helplessly watching the girl's ineffectual attempts to remove the pinkish stain from the skirt of her dress. Now that anger had caused her to drop her kittenish expression and manner, the girl looked a lot older. With an awful sinking feeling in the pit of her stomach,

Charlotte wondered if she had been mistaken about her age.

Mrs Clark got up from her seat and went around the table to place a comforting arm around the girl's shoulders. 'Now, now, calm down, Janice. It was an accident and it doesn't look all that bad. I'm sure it will come out in the wash if you soak it.'

'I always have this dress professionally dry-cleaned,' Janice informed her sulkily, giving Charlotte a baleful look.

'Of course, I'll pay for the cleaning,' Charlotte offered quickly, adding when her words had no effect on the other girl's expression, 'If the stain won't come out, I'll certainly pay for the dress.'

'I doubt if you could afford it,' Janice muttered petulantly, skimming over Charlotte's form with distaste.

Charlotte felt her temper rising, at war with her feelings of guilt. Certainly she'd been wrong to spill the drink, but really! The girl was acting like a rude, spoiled brat!

Charlotte was just about to do something very stupid that would undoubtedly cost her her job, when Harris intervened quickly, 'I think you've made your point now, Janice. It was an accident, so why not just forget it and go up and change?'

For a moment Janice looked inclined to argue, then she capitulated with a pout. 'Oh, OK, Harry, if you say so. Come on, Marian.'

Leaving the older woman to trail after her, she flounced from the room. Charlotte watched their progress until they were out of sight, then turned her attention back to the men at the table.

Her look of gratitude to Harris for curtailing the scene was met with a frigid stare. Chilled by it, she quickly shifted her attention to Mr Clark, saying, 'I really am sorry about that. I. . .er. . .'

'I guess these things happen,' he offered grudgingly, his displeasure scarcely hidden. 'It isn't as though you did it on purpose.'

Unable to reply to that, and with guilt firing her cheeks, Charlotte quickly leaned over the table and gathered up the crumpled napkins that littered it. From the corner of her eye, she slid a glance at Harris. He was watching her, his grey eyes hard as granite, his expression carved from that same unrelenting material. She swallowed to relieve the dryness in her throat, and quickly averted her gaze. She had an awful feeling he knew she hadn't spilled the drink accidentally, and a trickle of fear slithered down her spine.

'If you'll excuse me, I had best be getting back to work.' Just barely stopping herself from running, Charlotte escaped back to the bar.

As soon as she reached it, Tony demanded, 'What the hell were you doing over there?'

'It was an accident,' Charlotte lied defensively. 'I think she was under-age anyway. We could lose our licence serving drinks to minors, so it was just as well she had to leave.'

'Are you certain she was under-age?'

'Well. . .almost certain.'

'Well, next time, ask to see an ID instead of trying to drown the boss's girlfriend!'

'What do you mean? I didn't get any on Mrs Clark. Besides, that girl. . .' Charlotte came to a halt as an appalling idea entered her mind. She turned around to look at the table of two men, then back at Tony. 'Are you saying that Har—that that guy with Mr Clark is the new owner?'

'I thought you realised that.'

Charlotte gulped, feeling slightly sick. So, *Harris* was the new boss.

# CHAPTER TWO

IN THE break-room later, Charlotte sat staring at her evening meal, too engrossed in thought to be bothered finding an appetite for the simple fare of yoghurt, apple and crackers. She toyed with the paring knife she'd found in her lunch-bag, watching the play of light over its metallic blade as she thought about Harris.

His reaction tonight had surprised her. After all, what did he have to be bitter about? *He* was the one who had dumped her after they had spent the night together! She'd been heartbroken when she'd gone back to the ranch with her father and Harris hadn't got in touch with her. Finally, she had called him—several times, in fact. He had taken her calls, but he'd been cool, remote. So cool and remote that he could have been living at the South Pole and not just fifty miles away in Denver.

Charlotte had just been starting to accept the painful truth that he simply wasn't interested in continuing the relationship when she had found out that she was pregnant. For two weeks she'd lived in a private hell of her own, wondering what she was going to do, whom she could turn to. Then her father had found out.

She'd always been a little afraid of her father. She'd figured he would want to kill her when he found out she was 'in trouble'. His reaction had stunned her. He had seemed almost happy. Of course, he had known who the father was, as Charlotte had never dated anyone seriously but Harris.

When Mr Harper had insisted that Harris be told, Charlotte's feelings had been mixed. It didn't take a genius to figure out that her father's unexpected support was rooted in avarice. It might prove to be highly advantageous to him to be linked through marriage to a wealthy family.

Charlotte had had doubts about Harris's reaction, though. In recent weeks, he had made it pretty clear that, even if she saw their affair as the grand passion of her life, he didn't. It had been a brief interlude, a few laughs, and now it was over.

However, she had still been young enough and naïve enough to believe in happy endings. Once he found out she was pregnant, was carrying his child, surely Harris would have a change of heart, would realise that he loved her just as much as she loved him?

When they'd become engaged she had tried to convince herself that her future husband wasn't cast in that role simply because he figuratively had a gun held to his back. It hadn't been easy to maintain the fiction, though—impossible once she'd lost their baby.

The quiet snick of the door-latch sounded loud in the room, startling Charlotte out of her thoughts. Realising how odd she must appear, sitting alone in front of her untouched meal, she picked up the apple and lay the blade of the paring knife to its skin before turning her head to see who had come in.

Her hand stilled as she met Harris's eyes.

For several moments, their gaze held. Charlotte grew

conscious of the heavy beat of her heart within her chest, the tingling stir of awareness his presence awoke within her. Linda was right. Harris really was a hunk, she admitted, half disgusted with herself for still being drawn to him after all these years.

A full minute passed and still he didn't speak, so finally she said, 'Hello. . .Harris.' She said his name with a colouring of defiance. He'd prevented her from calling him by name earlier, stopped her from acknowledging that they knew one another. Now that they were alone, maybe he even thought she should call him 'Mr Jordan', since apparently he was now her boss.

'Charlie,' he acknowledged, nodding slightly. Charlotte flinched inwardly at the curt inflexion he placed on her name and quickly turned her attention back to the apple she was holding. It had been a private bond between them that they had both hated the diminutive of their names. Not that many people called him Harry, but everyone had always called her Charlie—except for Harris. He'd always used Charlotte because he'd known that was what she had preferred.

'It's been a long time,' she said inanely, the silence growing oppressive. She wasn't having much luck peeling the apple. Mangling it was more like it, but her hands wouldn't hold steady.

'Not long enough as far as I'm concerned. What are you doing here?' he demanded. He had moved to stand beside her and now his tall, hard-muscled body towered over her.

Resisting a feeling of intimidation, Charlotte glared up at him. 'Eating my supper?' she suggested with sugared insolence.

Anger clouded his features like cumulus building across a summer sky. 'That's not what I meant and you know it. I meant, what are you doing working here at my hotel?'

'A girl has to earn a living somehow.' Hacking at the apple, she sawed off a wedge and put it in her mouth. It was bitter, with an acid tang.

'I see,' Harris said severely, causing Charlotte to wonder just what he saw. He certainly didn't sound very understanding of the working class's need to put food on the table.

She slanted him a puzzled glance and received a stony glare in return. 'So what's it going to take to send you crawling back to the rock you came out from under?' he asked.

Although she knew she had been deliberately provocative, she was taken aback by his venom. 'What did you say?' she exclaimed, choking a little on the apple.

'You heard me. Don't play dumb. I caught that act years ago and you haven't improved on it. I want to know what I'm going to have to do to get you out of my life this time. You played havoc with it the last time—I don't think I'm ready for a rerun of that!'

Furious, Charlotte nearly choked on her apple. Slamming the remainder of the fruit down on the table, she swung around in her chair to face him, the paring knife clutched in her fist. 'You conceited bastard. You tore through my life like a hurricane, leaving nothing but chaos in your wake, and *you're* supposedly the one who's been hard done by!'

'As I recall, *you* were the one who broke off our engagement.'

'Don't tell me you've been nursing a broken heart over *that* all these years,' she scoffed. 'You know damn well you never wanted to marry me. I only did what was expected of me. If I hadn't called it off, you would have.'

It must have been a trick of the fluorescent lights overhead that made it appear that he had paled. He asked, his voice strangely hoarse, 'Is that why you did it?'

'Why else?'

Tears of fury misted her eyes and she blinked furiously to remove them before reaching for what remained of the apple. It would probably gag her, but she wasn't going to let him get to her.

As she hacked off a section of the fruit, Harris said softly, 'You shouldn't have done it. I didn't want that.'

Charlotte snorted. Who did he think he was kidding? 'Like hell. Look, it's all over with—in the past. Let's just forget it.'

She could feel him watching her as she forced down a bite of the apple. After several moments, he said, 'You're right, it is in the past. Right now, I'm concerned with the present. What was the big idea of dumping that drink all over Janice?'

Charlotte shrugged. 'It was an accident.'

'Was it? Are you sure it wasn't a case of the old green-eyed monster egging you on?'

'And what's that supposed to mean?'

He afforded her a considering look. 'Just that perhaps you were jealous of Janice for being with me. I seem to recall that was one of your biggest failings years ago.'

'Well, it's not "years ago" now, you conceited. . .baboon!' Charlotte sputtered. 'Your girlfriend's welcome to you!' As he continued to regard her with cool composure, her temper flared. 'She's welcome to *you*, but she isn't welcome in the bar. Obviously your tastes still run to teenagers, but don't expect me to wait on them. I happen to need this job and it won't be there if the Black Stallion is shut down for serving minors.' She slid him a look of derision. 'Although, it *is* your bar. Maybe you're so rich now, you don't care if it goes out of business.'

Ignoring her last thrust, he asked, 'Are you saying that you assumed Janice was under-age?'

'Well, she is, isn't she?' Charlotte retorted, stamping out the little doubts that flamed in her mind. She wished she had never brought the subject up. If only he hadn't accused her of being jealous! Why would he think she was jealous? Why *would* she be jealous?

'As a matter of fact, she isn't,' he told her smilingly. 'She'll be very flattered to know that you thought she was, though. Janice works very hard to project a youthful image.'

The implication being that *she* didn't, that she had let herself go until now she was nothing but an old hag. Charlotte looked away from him, staring at the container of yoghurt on the table. She'd probably be sick if she ate it. As it was, the apple wasn't sitting too well on her stomach. She resorted to playing with the paring knife.

'Well, you've told me off for spilling that drink on your girlfriend now, so if you've finished maybe you'll let me have my dinner in peace.'

She tuned her ears, hoping to hear him move away, but he only stepped closer, his bulk blocking the light and casting her in shadow as he rested his hands on the table and leaned over her. 'I haven't finished yet. You and I haven't seen each other for a long time—I wish it had been longer. You're a little complication from the past that I don't need turning up in my life right now.'

'So what am I supposed to do about that?' she asked.

'Disappearing would be nice. Quit your job here.'

'You really have a hell of a nerve,' she scorned, eyeing him with derision. 'Aside from anything else, I told you before, I need this job.'

'Find something else. I'll help you, if that's what you want.' His hand moved towards the inner pocket of his sports coat.

As she realised his intention, anger boiled through her veins, burning away the cold numbness. She stumbled to her feet, backing away from him. 'Keep your money! I don't need your or anybody else's charity. I work for my living! I work *here*. I'm sorry if I'm the skeleton that's fallen out of your closet, but I'm not quitting my job just for your convenience. You can fire me if you want me out of here—but if you do, we'll just see what the union has to say about it!'

'Calm down and be reasonable,' he enjoined. He'd taken his wallet out and held it in readiness. 'You'll not lose by quitting.'

'You be reasonable!' she shouted back at him, feeling cornered. She hated her job, hated the fresh customers, the smoke-filled atmosphere, the long hours on her feet, the skimpy uniform she was expected to wear. In other circumstances, she would have leapt at the chance to leave. But not on Harris's terms, not simply because her existence complicated his life! Didn't she have a right to live and breathe and carry on with her life without the almighty Harris Jordan's permission?

Her eyes were stony chips of amethyst as they met his grey stormy ones. For several moments they measured looks, then Harris moved his gaze to her hands, a look of puzzlement clouding his features.

Charlotte looked down. Crimson seeped from between the fingers of one clenched fist, collecting in rivulets that coursed across the back of her hand and fell in drops to the floor. The paring knife clattered to the floor when her fingers opened and blood streamed from a long, deep gash across her palm.

'Damn!' she muttered, pressing the palm of her uninjured hand against the wound to stem the flow of blood.

The sudden rush of pain up her arm caused her to gasp, and she clamped her lower lip between her teeth to stop herself from crying out. Harris was beside her then, slipping his arm around her shoulders and urging her towards the sink in the corner of the room.

Charlotte resisted him, saying, 'Don't fuss. Leave me alone and I'll put a Band-Aid on it.'

'A lot of good that will do,' he said grimly, then exploded with impatience as they reached the sink and he pulled her uninjured hand away from the wound. 'What an idiotic thing to do! What were you thinking, playing with the knife like that? You're going to need stitches, you know.' He turned on the taps and, after checking the temperature, grasped her cut hand and thrust it under the stream of water.

'I didn't do it on purpose,' Charlotte muttered. Her hand stung like fury as the water played over the wound and tears of pain clouded her eyes. Harris was right, she was an idiot to have done such a thing.

'Well, all I can say is that you're awfully accident-prone. I'm surprised you've survived all these years.'

'And don't you wish I hadn't?' she sniped. 'Then I wouldn't be a complication in your life now.'

'Stop talking nonsense.' He removed her hand from the water and started gently drying it with a paper towel. The water had temporarily stemmed the flow of blood, but it welled up again as he completed his task. Taking up a fresh towel, he folded it and pressed it over the wound, then curled her fingers over it to hold it in place.

'There must be a first-aid kit around here some place. We'll stick a bandage over it until I can get you to the hospital to get it stitched.'

'I can't go to the hospital,' Charlotte protested. She had stepped away from him and was cradling her injured hand against her midriff. Maybe that was where she should be, though—she must be sick. Even with everything that was going on, even with the throbbing pain of her wound as he had tended it, she had still been aware of his touch, the feel of his hands on her skin. They had set up a pulsating awareness of him that hurt almost as much as her injury.

His only answer was an exasperated look before he let his eyes roam about the room in search of the first-aid kit. Spying it at last, he retrieved it, and took it over to the table to open. 'Come here,' he ordered.

She supposed she would have to let him bandage her. The cut was on her right hand and she knew she couldn't manage it on her own. However, 'Look, I should have been back out in the bar five minutes ago. I don't have time to go to the hospital.'

'You're not working any more tonight,' Harris informed her as he taped a cotton-wool pad over the palm of her hand. I'll go tell the bartender what happened, then come back to fetch you.'

She gave him a frustrated look but, from the set of his features, decided further argument would be useless. She tried a different tack. 'What about your girlfriend? Won't she miss you? I'll get a taxi.'

He smiled at her mockingly. 'I'll drive you, but thanks for reminding me about Janice. I'll leave a message for her to let her know where I'm going.'

Gathering up the items he had removed from the box, he replaced them and closed the lid. As he turned to leave, she told him, 'Well, I'm not going out of here dressed like this!'

'Don't be ridiculous,' Harris enjoined. 'People who work at hospitals expect to see a little blood.'

Charlotte looked down at her uniform. The shining gold satin had been spattered with blood, but that wasn't why she couldn't possibly wear it outside the Black Stallion. The skirt was only about six inches long, barely covering the top of her thighs. It was also skin-tight, cutting across the top of her bosom to expose the ripe fullness of her breasts.

'You can't expect me to wear this outfit outside the bar! It's indecent!'

He gave her a long look. 'And that bothers you?'

Charlotte threw him a disgusted look and stalked over to her locker to retrieve her street clothes.

Harris watched her. When she turned back to him, he said, 'If the uniform bothers you so much, why wear it, why work here? Get a different kind of job. I just told you that I'd help out. Take me up on my offer.'

'Wouldn't you just love that?' Charlotte sneered, mustering her dignity as she strode over to the door of the dressing room. Pausing briefly, she turned to look at him. 'Quit worrying, Harris. Your dirty little secret's safe with me. I'm no more proud of that little episode than you are.'

Inside the safe haven of the dressing-room, Charlotte struggled to lower the back zip of her costume. It wasn't the easiest thing in the world to get out of at the best of times. Sometimes she wondered if it shouldn't be applied with a paintbrush—then she could use paint-remover to strip it off again! With only one hand available, her left one at that, it was proving nearly impossible to shed.

Giving the zipper tab an impatient tug, she heard the material give way as the fastener moved down a fraction. Shoot! She'd hoped to be changed before Harris got back—and to have found a taxi to drive her to the hospital. However, even though she hated her uniform, it wasn't worth ruining it simply to avoid her ex-fiancé. The waitresses at the Black Stallion were responsible for their own outfits and had to buy them from the management. Despite the fact that there wasn't much material in them, they weren't cheap. With luck and cold water, the blood stains would probably come out of this one and she could still wear it. However, it would be useless if she ripped the back out of it.

Taking a deep, calming breath, she started again, going more slowly this time. After several minutes, and a few curses, she managed to get the dress off. One-handed, she peeled her tights off and, wearing only brief bikini panties, turned around to find her bra. She hadn't heard the door open.

She froze to the spot, and her eyes met Harris's—met and clung. He wore a slightly stunned expression on his face, his face grey beneath his tan. Slowly, his eyes slid over her, his gaze almost a physical caress as he inspected the firm orbs of her breasts, the narrow curve of her waist, the feminine rounding of her hips.

Heat poured through her veins as she saw the flame kindle deep in his grey eyes, and yet she couldn't move. Time had no meaning. The moment might have spanned seconds or hours—past and present had merged.

Finally, though, she found her voice. 'What are you doing here?' she croaked.

Like a man in a dream, he shook his head, then stepped all the way into the tiny compartment, closing the door behind him. His nearness robbed her of the strength in her legs, leaving them shaken and weak. Striving for composure, she slowly picked up her T-shirt and held it in front of her.

'Don't, Charlotte,' he said quickly, softly, his hand automatically moving to grasp the top of the material. Their gaze entangled, he whispered, 'Please don't. Anything that lovely shouldn't be hidden. You have a perfect body, do you know that? You're even lovelier than I remembered.'

He didn't pull the material away but his hand lingered, burning into her flesh where he touched her. She should slap him, hit him, scream for help, but she couldn't move. He had removed his jacket and she could feel the heat emanating from his body. Knowing that the desire she read in his eyes was reflected in her own, she dropped them to stare at the crisp dark hairs that escaped from the open neck of his shirt.

'You shouldn't be in here. I'm trying to get dressed,' Charlotte said shakily.

He didn't reply. His hand insinuated itself beneath the shirt, moving down the side of her breast to cup its fullness. As his thumb toyed with the hard nub of her nipple, his other arm slid across her back, pulling her against him. He buried his face in the silken tumble of her blonde tresses, murmuring, 'You drive me crazy.'

In the back of her mind, Charlotte knew *she* must be crazy, and yet she felt herself melting against him. There had never been anyone in her life but Harris. Like a starving man suddenly confronted by a banquet, she wanted to gorge herself on his touch, his nearness. She rolled her head, exposing the smooth curve of her throat to him, drowning in the sensual touch of his mouth against her skin.

His hand feathered down her spine, slipping beneath the fragile nylon of her panties and splaying across her buttocks. As he drew her closer she could feel the hard urgency of his thighs and a shaft of questing passion darted through her.

'Harry, darling, are you in here?' The feminine tones

were muted as they drifted through the closed door, but they shattered the spell of sensuality none the less. Charlotte felt Harris tense as they listened to high-heeled shoes tapping out a staccato rhythm as someone moved around the break-room. A moment later, they heard the door close, then silence.

Charlotte stole a glimpse of his face. For a brief moment he looked as though he had been slapped, a dazed, stunned expression paralysing his features. Then, suddenly, he swore savagely under his breath and a second later he was pushing her away from him. Holding her off with his hands on her shoulders, he glared at her, self-condemnation twisting his mouth. 'You witch!' For a moment, she thought he was going to hit her but, after tightening their grip for a moment, his hands dropped to his sides. The T-shirt had fallen to the floor and he reached down and snatched it up. Thrusting it at her, he said savagely, 'For God's sake, get some clothes on.'

Charlotte held the crumpled shirt against her bosom. 'I didn't invite you in here.'

'You didn't exactly kick me out, either.'

That was true, she hadn't. Some crazy madness had overtaken her, addling her brain so that she welcomed his attentions. *He* had seduced her, though, not the other way around. 'Don't blame me for what happened! Besides, your *girlfriend* didn't know you were in here, so what are you so uptight about?' she mocked.

His expression was grim. 'Janice is not just my *girlfriend*,' he bit out. 'She happens to be the woman I'm going to marry. We've just gotten engaged—and after what just happened I think you ought to be able to see why I can't afford to have you around.'

Charlotte lowered her head, her eyes shielded behind her lashes. In recent years, she had more or less assumed that Harris had married. Most men did before they reached thirty. It shouldn't come as any shock then to find out he was engaged.

It had, though. That was how she felt—shocked. As though someone had just sent two thousand volts through her, leaving her stunned and lifeless.

'You. . .you're like some evil enchantress, robbing me of my senses.' He shook his head, self-disgust curling his mouth. 'I won't let this happen again—I can't. Now get dressed. I'll be waiting for you out in the bar. That hand still needs to be stitched.' He glanced at it. The taped bandage was still in place, but the cotton was tinged red where the wound had bled again.

'I'll take a cab,' Charlotte told him firmly.

'No, you won't. I'm taking you,' he insisted, his tone leaving no room for argument. He turned and left her alone.

# CHAPTER THREE

THE band was playing as Charlotte walked into the Black Stallion a few minutes later, the loud music hitting her like a physical blow. The lounge was more crowded than it had been earlier and several couples were on the dance-floor when she skirted it on her way to the bar, forcing her to side-step to avoid them. Her radar had picked out Harris and his fiancée sitting at the table where they had been before, so she kept her head averted. It would suit her fine if she never had to see or speak to him again. Maybe she shouldn't have let things get so out of hand in the dressing-room, but he couldn't lay all the blame at her door. She, at least, was free and heart-whole. *He* had a fiancée; *he* had started it all by coming in on her in the first place.

When she reached the bar, Tony came over to her. She said, 'I'm sorry to have put you on the spot like this. It was a stupid accident.'

'Don't worry about it. Mr Jordan arranged for someone from the coffee-shop to come fill in for you.' Trust Harris to take over, Charlotte thought bitterly, not appreciating Tony's reminder as to who was now their boss.

When she didn't reply, he glanced down at her hand. 'Don't you think you ought to be getting that thing taken care of? It must hurt like hell.'

'It does, actually.' Charlotte grimaced. Maybe that

was why she felt a little sick when she felt Harris come up behind her. She didn't want to face him, but she forced herself to turn around.

His fiancée was with him, hanging on to his arm as if it were a lifeline. In the brighter lights around the bar, Charlotte could see how wrong she had been about her age. Her face wasn't devoid of cosmetics, but it was so expertly made-up that it was only in the more intense light that one could see the flaws it concealed. She had changed out of her soiled dress and into another, although it too was cut along juvenile lines. However, Charlotte wasn't deceived this time. Harris's fiancée, she suspected, was closer to thirty than the seventeen or eighteen she had originally placed her as.

'You ready to go?' Harris's curt question curtailed her inspection of his companion.

'Yes, but you don't have to drive me. There are usually cabs parked out in front of the lobby. I'll get Murray to get me one.'

'I said I'd drive you and I will.'

Charlotte gave him a look of dismayed exasperation. Harris could be exceptionally pig-headed! She looked at his fiancée. She didn't look any happier about Harris's insistence than Charlotte felt.

'Darling, if—er—Charlie,' Janice smiled over at her, 'would rather take a cab——'

'I'm driving her,' Harris persisted stubbornly. 'And I think we ought to quit arguing about it and get moving.'

He reached out to grasp Charlotte's elbow to escort her from the lounge and his fiancée said with irritation, 'But, Harry. . .'

Charlotte wondered if it annoyed him as it did her to hear Janice call him that. Perhaps. His tone was certainly sharp enough when he told the other woman, 'Janice, I don't want to discuss it any more.'

His fiancée gave him a startled look and Charlotte saw Harris bite his lower lip. 'I'm sorry, honey. I didn't mean to snap. Look, this won't take long and I'll see you in your room when I get back.' He looked down at her, his smile coaxing and promising all sorts of things for later on. Janice tossed Charlotte a somewhat bewildered look, then looked back at her fiancé. She tipped her head up to him and he dropped a light kiss on to her parted lips. His head close to hers, he whispered something Charlotte couldn't catch. However, when Janice turned back to look at her, the disgruntled look was gone from her face and she was purring.

'Whatever you say, darling.'

A look of satisfaction on his face, Harris redirected his attention to Charlotte, urging her from the room. As they walked through the brightly lit lobby towards the exit, Charlotte remarked, 'If I were your fiancée and you had talked to me like that just before going off with another girl, you sure wouldn't find me welcoming you to my room when you got back! All that lovey-dovey sop wouldn't have worked, either.'

'But then, you're not my fiancée any more. Maybe that's why,' Harris said coldly as he held the door for her.

As Charlotte stepped from the air-conditioned building into the warm night air she felt none the less chilled. He really liked to rub it in, didn't he? Well, she'd die before she let him know that it bothered her!

When they reached the car, she paused as he held the door open for her. Looking straight into his eyes, she said, 'All those years ago, I was so desperately in love with you that I was always fretting about what I could do to make you love me back. It never occurred to me that what I really needed to do was turn myself into a doormat so that you could wipe your feet all over me— thank God! I might have been young enough and stupid enough to try it. Janice is welcome to you—but I do feel sorry for her.' With that, she slid into the passenger seat and pulled the door closed.

When Harris joined her, sliding in behind the wheel of the big Cadillac, his mouth was set in a harsh line. 'Janice is not my doormat and, even if she were, it wouldn't be any of your business. As for loving me all those years ago. . .' He slewed around in his seat to look at her with hard granite eyes. He said brutally, 'I'll admit you went to considerable lengths to get me to propose marriage, but somehow I don't think love played any part of it. Tell me, how is your father's cattle business faring these days? Is he still using you as bait to sell his beef?'

He leaned over and switched on the ignition. As he waited for a break in the traffic before turning out of the car park he continued, 'I'll give you this. You certainly taught me a lesson every young man should learn—always call a bluff. What a coincidence that no sooner had your father discovered he wasn't going to be able to fleece his future in-laws than the wedding was off.'

It truly had been a coincidence, though Charlotte didn't bother telling Harris so. She had broken her ties

with her father all those years ago, so it mattered little
now. He'd been furious with her for sending Harris
back his ring. It was only then that she had learned of
the business deal he'd hoped to cook up with his future
in-laws. He'd wanted them to finance a feed-lot oper-
ation that he would control, then further provide a
ready market for the finished beef in their hotels. He'd
blamed her broken engagement for the failed plan—
ironic, after all these years, to find out that that hadn't
been the cause for his deal's going sour after all.

Not that it would have changed things. Bitterly
disillusioned, she would have left anyway, although
maybe she would have felt more as if she was walking
away from her father than that he was throwing her
out. Preoccupied with his business setbacks, he'd completely ignored the fact that his daughter had just been
through an emotional wringer: physically and mentally
wounded by a miscarriage, her marriage plans
dropped. All he'd cared about was that his dreams of
making a fortune by way of the Jordans had ended.
Knowing that her father had been using her, that his
warm sympathy when he'd discovered her pregnancy
had only been a sham, had further undermined
Charlotte's state of mind.

'Nothing to say for yourself?' Harris asked harshly
as her silence filled the car. She turned to look at him,
taking in the bitter set of his mouth even when viewed
in profile. Odd that he should be so bitter about the
past. He'd come through the whole stinking mess
relatively unscathed. It had taken her years to get back
on balance, to put it all behind her. Sometimes, she
wondered if she had managed to even yet.

'Is that why you insisted on driving me to the hospital? So we could argue, so you could throw charges at me and rake up ancient history?' she asked wearily.

He didn't answer immediately, but concentrated his attention on steering the big car into the hospital car park. Finding a free space, he drove the car into it and braked. In the silence after the motor ceased, he turned to her, studying her features in the pale light cast by the street-lamp. 'No, it isn't why I wanted to drive you,' he admitted at last. 'I didn't intend to argue. Maybe I *did* want to make you feel a little guilty, hit on some vein of your better nature. Can't you see how impossible it is for you to continue working at the Foothills now that I own it?'

They were back to that again. She couldn't argue with his assertion, though. As she looked at him, she could feel a treacherous yearning growing within her. He was a dangerous man for her. She'd read somewhere that heroin addicts never completely lost their craving for the drug, that years later they still remained susceptible. She could believe it. After all this time, she knew she could make as big a fool of herself over him as she had when she was seventeen.

Why hadn't he stayed away? What trick of fate had caused him to buy this hotel when there must be hundreds of hotels in Colorado? She was settled here, her life a well-drawn map. There was something unfair in his thinking she should be the one to make sacrifices, to uproot. 'So I'm supposed to quit. I don't imagine it has occurred to you that *you* could sell the hotel again. I was there first.'

'It took me months of negotiations to buy it. I've started the ball rolling to move the headquarters of Jordan's into the upper floors.' He shook his head. 'It would be much simpler for *you* to quit.'

She was fighting a losing battle and she knew it. Weariness assailed her and the throbbing in her hand seemed to grow acutely worse all at once. She leaned back in her seat rubbing her temple with her uninjured hand. 'Do we have to talk about this now? I thought the idea of driving all this way was so that I could get my hand fixed up.'

He saw the tired droop of her shoulders and immediately concern softened the stern lines of his features. 'I'm sorry, Charlotte. You're right, we can talk tomorrow.' He got out of the car and went around it to help her from her seat. 'Look, maybe I should carry you?' he suggested as she staggered slightly upon standing.

Getting her balance, Charlotte stared at him. To have those strong, secure arms around her, to be held against that firm, muscular chest; she almost laughed aloud at the very idea. Didn't he *know* what kind of effect that would have on her? He wasn't immune to her either, she knew, remembering that scene in the dressing-room. Being in his arms would be playing with fire for both of them.

Quickly, Charlotte turned away and started walking towards the brightly lit entrance to the emergency ward before she did something even more foolish than cutting her hand.

Harris had brought her to a very efficient hospital. It seemed no time at all before the gash on her palm was neatly closed with three stitches, her hand swathed in a gauze bandage. They had 'frozen' her hand in order to stitch it so that she didn't even feel the wound now. In case it bothered her later on that night, she had been given a small vial of pain-killers to ease the ache.

As she stood at the reception counter some time later, studying the methodically laid out bill for service, she wished the accounts department didn't emulate the hospital's general competence to such a degree. Who would have thought such a simple procedure would have cost so much to perform?

She looked up and found a winning smile for the waiting receptionist. 'Would it be possible to have you bill me through the mail?' Charlotte asked sweetly.

The girl frowned. 'We'd prefer you to settle it now.' On seeing Charlotte's disgruntled expression, she supplied, 'If there's a problem you can come back in the morning and discuss it with one of the supervisors. They might be able to arrange a payment schedule.'

'Well. . .' Charlotte bit her lip. She'd always avoided the trap of monthly payments, preferring to pay as she went. There was some money in her savings account and if she tightened her belt this next pay period she could probably manage the bill. Reaching into her handbag for her cheque-book, she just hoped that the accounts department weren't as speedy at cashing cheques as they were at drawing up statements, because she would have to transfer money into her account to cover it.

She hadn't taken her wallet out when Harris came up behind her.

'So here you are. I went down to the cafeteria for a coffee, and when I got back you'd disappeared.'

Well, so much for slipping out of the hospital and getting a cab home. Perhaps it was just as well, though, she thought, taking another look at the total on the bill. She wasn't going to be able to afford taxis for a while.

Harris was looking over her shoulder at the bill as well. She didn't notice him reach into the inner pocket of his sports jacket as she rummaged through her bag for her cheque-book, but when she looked back he had *his* cheque-book out and was writing in it.

'What do you think you're doing?' she demanded.

'I'm paying the bill,' he said, not pausing as he filled in the amount and started signing the cheque.

'I pay my own bills, thank you,' Charlotte said firmly, slapping her own book on the counter and picking up a pen to write in it.

Ignoring her, Harris finished signing his signature before looking over to her. 'Look, I feel responsible for what happened. If we hadn't have been arguing. . .'

'It was my fault, none the less. I don't want you paying my bills.' Considering the matter closed, she began writing out the cheque. She was aware of Harris's eyes on her as she did so and it made her nervous. As it was, it wasn't that easy to write with her bandaged hand, still numb from the local anaesthetic. She botched the first cheque. Tearing it out with a grunt of irritation, she filled out another, concentrating mightily to complete the task. Finally, it was done acceptably and she pulled the cheque out of the book.

Before she could hand it over, Harris stepped closer

to her, half turning from the counter so his back was to the clerk. In an undertone, he asked, 'Don't you think you ought to let me pay this?'

'I said I'd take care of it,' Charlotte reminded him, vexed. 'I don't need your charity.'

'Don't you?' he asked sceptically, sliding his gaze to her still open cheque-book. Charlotte's eyes followed his, her lips tightening as she realised what he was looking at. She believed in keeping meticulous records, making sure that she would always know to the penny the amount in her bank account. It was right there in black and white—and nowhere near enough to cover the cheque she'd just written!

And snoopy old Harris knew it, too!

'It'll be OK,' she muttered, pushing past him to the counter and handing the receptionist the cheque. She knew he was watching her with exasperation as she waited for the receptionist to stamp her invoice 'paid'. As soon as the girl handed it over to her, she turned on her heel and stalked towards the exit.

Just outside the door, Harris caught up with her. Keeping pace with her, he asked, 'You do know that it's illegal to write a short cheque, don't you? That one's going to bounce all the way to the bank!'

'It's none of your business, but the cheque *won't* bounce. I have some money in my savings account. I just have to transfer it over.'

'You're sure about that?' he asked doubtfully. Charlotte didn't reply but, quickening her pace, kept her eyes fixed on the car they were heading towards. Her cheeks were faintly warm. There wasn't *quite*

enough in her account, but if she made good tips this
weekend she should be all right.

She had to wait for him to unlock the passenger door
for her when they got to the car. As he slipped the key
into the lock, he asked bluntly, '*Do* you have enough
in savings to cover that cheque?'

She tossed him a fed-up look. 'Would you just stop
sticking your big nose in my financial affairs? It has
nothing to do with you.' Without waiting for him to
open the door for her, she pulled it open and threw
herself into the front seat. With a violent jerk, she
slammed the door and the car rocked.

Harris glared at her through the window for a
moment, then marched around the front of the car to
take his place behind the wheel.

Inside the car, he reached into his pocket and pulled
out a roll of notes. Pushing them at her, he ordered,
'Take this and put it in your current account
tomorrow.'

'I'm not taking your money!'

He gave her a hard, furious look and she quailed
slightly. The tense silence filled the tiny space in the
vehicle, then he dropped the notes into her lap, saying,
'Take it. Consider it an advance on your salary. I'll
make sure that it's taken off your next pay-cheque.'

Mutinously, Charlotte stared down at the crumpled
notes in her lap. Without giving her an opportunity to
argue further, Harris started the car up and drove to
the exit of the car park. 'Which way?' he asked curtly.

Charlotte gestured to the right. When he had pulled
the car on to the street, she asked sulkily, 'You'll make
sure it comes off my cheque?'

'I'll make sure.'

She swallowed hard. 'Well, then. . .er. . .thank you,' she allowed grudgingly. She picked up the notes and smoothed the wrinkles from them before putting them into her bag. They really would come in handy. She could admit to herself now that she would have had to make some pretty fabulous tips this weekend if she had had to depend on them to make up that hospital bill. As long as it was coming out of her wages, she supposed there was nothing wrong with taking the money.

They had been driving for a few minutes, with Charlotte silently gesturing directions to her apartment, when something occurred to her. 'I thought you wanted me to quit my job at the Black Stallion? If I do, how will I pay back the money you've lent me?'

He didn't answer immediately—it was apparently an aspect of the situation he hadn't considered. After a quick glance at his profile, Charlotte reached for her handbag and opened it to retrieve the notes.

'Oh, for Pete's sake don't let's go through all that again!' he exclaimed when he realised what she was up to. 'Keep the money. . .keep the damn job, for that matter! It's a big hotel. . .we'll just stay out of each other's way!'

'I. . .er. . .' Charlotte didn't know what to reply. Now that he had relented on her keeping her job, she found herself longing to leave. How could it possibly work? Granted, the Foothills was a big complex, but it had a small-town atmosphere. Everyone knew what everyone else was doing, and gossip, particularly about the bosses, was rife. Was she going to be able to take hearing a blow-by-blow account of Harris's life every day? Harris's and *Janice's* lives? Much as she wished she could deny it, she knew she was jealous of the girl. In the bar earlier, when Harris had kissed his fiancée, it had been like a knife twisting in her heart. She could just picture Linda coming in every evening, bubbling over with all the petty details of the wedding preparations—all the nights that they shared a room.

She looked out through the windscreen and saw the street she lived on coming up. 'Turn here, it's the third house on the right.' As he did as she bade, Charlotte said quietly, 'I'll be looking for another job. I'm not sure how I'll pay you back the money, but don't worry, I will.'

Harris slid the car into a parking slot in front of the old Victorian building that housed her apartment. Twisting off the key, he shrugged, 'Suit yourself.'

His hand went to the door-handle and Charlotte said quickly, 'You don't have to see me to the door.' Without waiting for a reply, she scrambled out on to the pavement. Harris, however, had ignored her words and joined her a moment later.

'I don't like the idea of a woman going into an empty apartment late at night by herself,' he explained, escorting her up the path.

'I do it most nights—although the apartment is rarely empty.'

They had reached the door to her apartment by now and the blare of the television set coming through the door lent support to her words.

'I hadn't realised you lived with another girl.'

'Not a girl,' Charlotte said simply, and she saw his

eyes stray to her ringless finger. 'And no, I'm not married.'

'But you're living with a man, is that what you're trying to say?' he asked evenly.

'Got it in one.' She turned to slide her key into the lock. She knew what he was thinking, she knew she'd deliberately given him a totally erroneous picture of her and Jimmy's relationship. It made her feel better, though. She didn't want him thinking she had spent these past few years pining over him—he certainly hadn't pined; he had Janice. She hadn't either, but he might not believe that if he knew there hadn't been anyone else in her life but him. Letting him think there was salvaged her pride somehow.

By the time she had the door open, Harris was gone.

## CHAPTER FOUR

THE only light in the room came from the large colour television flickering in one corner. The volume was turned too high and Charlotte winced as the raucous sound beat against her eardrums. The neighbours would be complaining again—although Jimmy would probably ignore them as usual. Smiling wryly at the man snoring peacefully in the reclining armchair, she walked over to the set and turned it off. Not for diamonds would Jimmy admit he was getting a little hard of hearing. The one and only time she had brought it up, suggesting that he might consider wearing a hearing-aid, he had become so angry that she'd been forced to let the subject drop.

The sudden silence was loud in the small apartment and, turning to survey the clutter, Charlotte wrinkled her nose in distaste at the stale odour of cigarette smoke. The ashtray on the table next to the chair was overflowing with butts and she pursed her lips in exasperation. Jimmy was always falling asleep in that chair, and she expected to come home one of these nights to find he'd burned the place down through nodding off with a cigarette still burning. It was downright dangerous.

Walking to the table, she picked up the ashtray to clean it out. As she turned to leave, the old man stirred then suddenly sat upright.

'Where have you been?' he demanded, his china-blue eyes still blurred with sleep, the over-long white fringe that edged his bald pate tousled.

'I was at work. I've just come in,' Charlotte explained patiently, the question not surprising her as it might once have. Jimmy didn't remember the day-to-day happenings in life very well any more. It was funny really. He could recall some incident from fifty years ago with complete and astounding clarity, but ask him about something that had occurred only that day and he drew a blank. It was as though some incompetent secretary had played havoc with his memory files, misfiling the present and recent past where he couldn't find them.

And it made him angry. Blunt and outspoken, Jimmy had never been anyone's idea of sweet old man, but lately—she could see the confusion in his eyes, see the helpless fury as he realised he should have known where she had been.

'I'll make us some coffee,' she offered quickly, wanting to avert an explosion. When he couldn't remember, he had to blame someone—and she was the only one available.

Without waiting for an answer, Charlotte escaped to the kitchen. As the door closed behind her, she heard the television roar to life. Trying not to think about what the neighbours must be saying, she went to the cupboard and took out the coffee things. The kitchen was bright and cheerful—she'd spent one summer vacation painting it a warm buttercup-yellow and sewing gingham curtains for the windows. The linoleum was old and worn in spots, though, the porcelain sink chipped, the wooden cupboards old-fashioned. Some-times, Charlotte thought about moving to an apartment in a newer building, one where the plumbing didn't groan and the furnace always worked. Jimmy liked this place, though—said it reminded him of the house he had grown up in.

She guessed that it wasn't so bad after all, if it made him happy. He was over eighty, and he deserved happiness in his final years. Charlotte felt she owed it to him. Once, when she had been bitterly unhappy, he had practically saved her life.

It had been shortly after she'd left home. What little savings she'd taken with her were nearly depleted, and she'd had no luck finding a job. Worse than that, though, was that she hadn't seemed able to care about the straits she had been in. Ever since losing her baby and breaking her engagement, she'd been depressed, but by then it had been almost to the point of debili-tation. The seedy hotel where she'd been living had been about to throw her out for non-payment of rent, she hadn't had a decent meal in days—and she simply hadn't cared. She had spent her days in the park, spending precious dimes she couldn't afford buying breadcrumbs to feed overweight pigeons.

It had been there that she had met Jimmy. She'd seen the elderly man around the last few days, but he'd been too much in the background for him to impinge much on her consciousness. He had come to share her bench that day, though, and after a few minutes of silence had asked in what she was later to discover was his typically forthright manner, 'What's a fine, healthy young woman like yourself doing hanging around the park every day? Why aren't you in school or working—or are you one of them drop-outs?'

Charlotte ignored him. Why did the elderly seem to think that, just because they'd lived longer than everyone else, they could be as rude and bothersome as they liked?

'I asked you a question, young lady—or don't you have the courtesy to answer me?'

He was a fine one to talk about courtesy! However, Charlotte replied, 'If you must know, I've graduated from high school now and I just haven't been able to find a job.'

He gave her a hard look. 'You think one of them fat old birds is going to give you one? Feeding pigeons is for old men like me, not strong young things like yourself.'

Charlotte eyed him with annoyance, her anger building out of all proportion. It was months since she had felt any emotion. It was almost as if she lived in an invisible bubble of apathy, tough and resilient and impenetrable. Today, though, this uncouth, crotchety old man had pierced it. Suddenly she shoved the half-filled bag of crumbs at him, saying, 'Well, then, you can feed them—just leave me alone.' Getting to her feet, she stalked away.

She stayed away from the park for a full week. She even went out looking for a job, a different place to live. She didn't have much luck with either, though, and she ended up at the park again, once again swamped by depression and not giving a damn what happened to her.

The old man was there again.

It was an uneasy alliance in the beginning, but they were drawn together because they needed each other. Charlotte needed someone to care about her because she didn't care about herself, and Jimmy—he was old, he was alone in the world—he simply needed someone to care for. . .

When Charlotte carried the coffee back into the living-room, she found that Jimmy had dropped off again. His head was thrown back, his mouth gaping, his loud snoring competing with the din from the television. She turned the set off again and, taking a seat on the worn sofa, blew on her coffee for a moment before taking a sip.

She was tempted to wake Jimmy, then thought better of it. He would be upset about her cut hand—it was starting to throb now—and she didn't feel like going into long explanations at this time of night. Besides, she might be tempted to tell about seeing Harris again.

Jimmy knew all about Harris. She'd told him the whole sorry story a few months after they'd first met. She'd welcomed his support at that time—he'd been totally biased in her favour, condemning the man he considered had 'taken advantage' of her. Jimmy had an old-fashioned outlook on life, and didn't condone premarital sex. On hearing her story, he had cast Harris in the role of the black-hearted villain. The situation hadn't been quite that cut and dried, although it was probably wiser to let him see things that way than have him cast her in the role of fallen woman.

Knowing his bias, though, she wasn't sure she wanted to discuss Harris's reappearance in her life with him just yet. Her feelings about it, about Harris, were a confused tangle. She needed to sort them out in her own mind, without outside interference, before discussing her ex-fiancé with anyone.

Charlotte finished her coffee and set the cup aside. Her hand was hurting like mad now. She got up from the couch and picked up the afghan draped across its back to cover Jimmy with it. Finding her handbag, she took out the pain-killers and swallowed one before turning out the lights and going to bed.

'Charlie!' Linda charged up as soon as Charlotte stepped into the lounge the next evening. 'How'd your date with Mr Jordan go last night?'

Charlotte treated her to a disbelieving look, shaking her head slightly. She was also annoyed. This place was a regular Peyton Place. It had been pure wishful thinking to suppose that her accident last night and subsequent ride to the hospital wouldn't be the main topic on the grapevine today. 'Since when is a ride to the emergency ward a date?' she asked petulantly, stepping around the girl to go to the bar.

'But he did take you,' Linda persisted, trailing after her and fairly panting with curiosity. 'Did he wait and drive you home afterwards?'

'Yes,' Charlotte snapped, signalling to Tony to bring her her float. She hadn't any patience for Linda tonight. She hadn't slept very well the previous night and, while she would have liked to blame it on her injured hand, the pain pills had worked marvellously. Unfortunately, they hadn't been able to turn off her thoughts. Consequently, she'd overslept and hadn't had time to look for another job as she'd intended.

'Did he ask you out again?' the younger girl demanded just as Tony came up. Ignoring Linda, Charlotte accepted the money the bartender handed her and began counting it. Undaunted, Linda continued, 'I wish I could get him to notice me. He's just about the most fabulous guy I've ever seen. You were really lucky to have cut your hand when he was here.'

Somehow, Charlotte managed to get her float counted despite Linda. However, she couldn't let the girl's last remark pass unanswered. 'Look, Linda, I didn't feel very lucky at the time and I still don't. Besides, I wouldn't get too infatuated with Mr Jordan if I were you—he's engaged.'

Linda looked devastated. 'He is?' She looked hard at Charlotte, then pronounced, 'Oh, he can't be. I would have heard about it!'

'You're hearing about it now,' Charlotte said drily, scooping up her tray and walking off. She didn't enjoy gossip, and garnered scant satisfaction from being the first in with news for a change, but at least maybe now Linda would shut up about Harris!

When Charlotte returned to the bar with her orders, to her relief, Linda was out on the floor taking care of her own customers. However, she didn't escape the awkward questions. As Tony was mixing her drinks, he asked, 'OK, so what's the scoop really on Mr Jordan?'

'No scoop, Tony. As I told Linda, he's engaged—to that girl that was in here with him last night.'

'But what about you and him?' he persisted.

'What about us? He drove me to the hospital, drank the lousy coffee in the cafeteria and drove me home,' Charlotte said defensively. 'You're as bad as Linda—how can you make anything out of that?'

He set a frosted cocktail on her tray and filled another glass with ice. Working as he spoke, he continued, 'Put that way, not much—except I think there was more to it than that. He came back to the bar afterwards and was asking about you—you and Jimmy. He seemed to have the impression that you two were shacked-up. I thought you only used that line when you were trying to get rid of some guy?'

Tony only had one more drink to mix and Charlotte wished he would get on with it. He was deliberately being slow, though, so that she would be forced to answer him. Finally, she said, 'Well, maybe I wanted to get rid of him!'

'But you just said he was engaged. Why would you need to turn him off?' He set the last drink on her tray. 'There's something fishy going on here and I wish you would let me in on it. Did you know him before?'

Charlotte would dearly have loved to pick up her tray and simply walk away. Unfortunately, Tony wasn't in the same category as Linda—he was more than a co-worker, he was a very dear friend. 'Tony. . .yes, I know him, but. . .I really can't explain.' The bartender gave her a thoughtful look and her eyes were apologetic. 'Just. . .you didn't tell him the truth about Jimmy, did you?'

He shook his head. 'You know I wouldn't do that without talking it over with you first.'

'Thanks and. . .let him go on thinking whatever he wants.'

'Are you sure? He seemed. . .' He hesitated, searching for the right word, then continued, 'He seemed awfully concerned about you last night. He had a lot of questions about Jimmy. . .almost as if he were checking him out to see if he was good enough for you.'

'He wasn't being concerned. . .just nosy,' Charlotte dismissed her friend's words. 'Why would he be concerned, anyway? He really is engaged to that girl.'

Tony shrugged. 'Well, if you say so.'

'I do.' Taking up the tray of drinks, Charlotte went to serve her customers.

It was around ten o'clock when Harris walked in with Janice on his arm. Linda had already left for the night as she sometimes worked an earlier shift, so Charlotte had no choice but to wait on the couple. They took a table near the bar and reluctantly she walked up to them.

'Good evening,' she greeted them, not quite able to keep the dismay from her tone. She'd thought she and Harris had agreed to avoid one another. 'What can I get for you tonight?'

Harris's eyes were steely. 'How's your hand?' he asked harshly. 'I thought you might take a few days off to give it a chance to heal.' He didn't need to add that he would have found somewhere else to take his fiancée for a drink if he'd known Charlotte would be here. His manner said it for him.

'It's OK,' Charlotte told him. Actually, her hand bothered her quite a bit, but she needed to work.

However, now didn't seem to be the time for enlightening Harris on the shabby benefits the Foothills provided their employees with despite their union. The management might feel sorry for you if you were sick, but they still didn't pay you if you didn't come in.

She gave the girl an encouraging look, hoping to take the order as quickly as possible so she could escape. Janice obliged her. 'I'll just have coffee,' she ordered, then smiled over at her escort. 'We had wine at dinner so I don't want anything more to drink. You go ahead and have whatever you want, though.'

Despite her invitation, Charlotte noticed she looked disapproving when Harris ordered a double Scotch. Charlotte suspected he needed a boost of whisky—when she'd seen him come into the lounge, she had felt like having one herself—but his fiancée apparently felt it a bit much at this stage of the evening.

As Charlotte moved the few feet back to the bar, she was beginning to wonder if Janice wasn't something of a prude. She'd noticed the girl eyeing Annabelle, the nude over the bar, with a faintly scandalised expression. Also, while pink squirrels were alcoholic, they were also the kind of drink one might recommend to a non-drinker as they didn't taste boozy. Janice certainly dressed conservatively, if somewhat childishly. If Janice was very puritanical, it would explain why Harris was so set on keeping his past hidden.

Charlotte picked up her tray with their order on it and turned back to the table. She was frowning slightly. Her theory might have held water, if she hadn't heard Harris promise to go to his fiancée's room last night. It had been pretty clear he wasn't going up there to read the Bible with her!

She was setting the coffee in front of Janice when the phone rang and Tony hailed her from the bar. 'Charlie, it's for you.'

'Just a second.' Hastily she transferred the glass of Scotch from her tray to the table in front of Harris. 'Do you want to run a tab?' she asked.

Harris hadn't had a chance to answer when Tony called again, 'Charlie, I think you had better get over here and take this.'

She looked over her shoulder at the bartender and he held the phone out to her. He looked a little harried. Uncertainly, she looked back at Harris. 'Take your call. We'll wait,' he offered sardonically.

'Thank you,' Charlotte said quickly and walked back to the bar, aware of the couple's eyes riveted on her. 'What was the big panic?' she hissed at Tony, taking the receiver from him. Personal phone calls weren't encouraged and this one couldn't have come at a worse time—right in the middle of waiting on Harris, her boss.

'It's Jimmy,' Tony explained apologetically. 'I tried talking to him but. . .he's pretty upset.'

Charlotte's brow wrinkled in puzzlement, she spoke into the receiver. 'Hello?'

A stream of curses greeted her and automatically she moved the phone away from her ear. Something had set the old man off but she wasn't going to be able to find out what it was until he'd calmed down.

She was trying to figure a way of getting a word in edgewise so she could do just that, when she realised that Harris had come up to the bar and was standing right beside her. One glance at his stony expression told her he could hear the abusive language coming out of the phone. Her face scorching, she moved the phone closer to her ear and half turned away from Harris.

'Calm down, Jimmy!' she enjoined in a harsh undertone. The injunction didn't do her much good and another minute passed before the old man simmered down enough for her to make out what the problem was. In the meantime, she was acutely conscious of Harris's steel-grey eyes boring into her back.

'There's almost a full carton in the cupboard by the sink where I always put them,' Charlotte explained. Jimmy had run out of cigarettes and couldn't find any more. At the old man's response, she admitted, 'Yes, I know I used to keep them there, but I changed things around, remember?' He didn't, that was the whole trouble. Finally he was placated, and she hung up the phone, nibbling her lip as she did so. It had been almost a *year* since she had rearranged the kitchen cupboards in a fit of housecleaning. Poor Jimmy—just pray to God he didn't burn the building down now that he had his 'smokes' again.

She glanced up to find Harris studying her. 'I seem to recall you taking me to task once for the way I spoke to Janice,' he reminded her sardonically.

Charlotte flushed uncomfortably. 'This is a different situation,' she muttered.

'It sure sounds like it,' he said disgustedly, picking up the creamer and sugar bowl he'd come to the bar to fetch. Chagrined—she should have brought those with the coffee—Charlotte watched him go back to his table, then relucantly followed him.

He gave her an unwelcoming look of enquiry when she reached his seat. 'Er. . .we didn't settle what you were going to do about the bill.'

'I usually run a monthly tab at my hotels,' he informed her coldly. Charlotte nodded and turned to make her escape back to the bar. He forestalled her, 'Also, in my hotels. . .' he was really hammering it home as to who the boss was, Charlotte decided, frost-bitten by his tone of voice '. . .in *my* hotels, I don't encourage employees to take personal phone calls during working hours. You might want to let your "friend" know that for future reference.'

Charlotte didn't have an opportunity to go looking for another job until Monday morning. She'd had the previous day off and Jimmy had woken up in such a good frame of mind, so much like his old self, that she'd scrapped her job-hunting plans and coaxed her elderly Volkswagen into taking them for a drive in the mountains.

As a young man, Jimmy had worked in the Rockies, mining for silver and gold. He had a wealth of stories and kept Charlotte thoroughly entertained throughout the day. It had been a precious day, had formed a precious memory to store away. With his advancing senility and eighty-five years, she knew she had to savour the good days when they happened.

Monday was a day of pounding the pavement and making futile enquiries, though. By the late afternoon, discouragement more than actual fatigue left Charlotte feeling exhausted. Boulder was a university town, which meant there was a surfeit of casual labour available in the summer, but as the spring term had ended a few weeks earlier most of the openings for summer staff had already been filled.

Trudging back to the car park where she had left her car, Charlotte realised she had only had one job offer to show for her day, and she didn't think she was desperate enough to accept it. Just thinking about the place made her skin crawl. The Black Stallion might not be the grandest place in the world to work at, but at least it didn't smell of beer and stale cigarette smoke and urine. And whatever else one could say about the uniforms, they were at least clean, she admitted, recalling the bartender of the tavern that had offered her work. Of course, maybe he never washed his clothes because they were so old that they'd fall apart if he did!

She was halfway home when she realised she hadn't checked the work schedule on Saturday night and so she didn't know what shifts she was supposed to work this week. Grimacing, Charlotte turned down a side-street to head back towards the centre of town and the Foothills. She would have preferred to avoid the hotel and Harris, but as it was the only job it appeared she was going to have this summer she'd better make an effort to hang on to it.

Diane, the hotel secretary, was just sliding the cover over her typewriter when Charlotte walked into the office. 'Just leaving?' she asked, going over to the bulletin board to check the work schedule.

'In a couple of minutes,' Diane affirmed, though she

gave Charlotte a somewhat puzzled look. Charlotte herself was looking very puzzled when she turned back to the other girl.

'My name has been crossed off the schedule. What's going on?'

'I was wondering what you were doing here. Mr Jordan came in this morning and told me to rework the schedule because you'd quit—he said you'd found another job.'

'He said that?' Charlotte demanded, outraged at his gall. He'd told her she could keep her job—how dared he fire her now?

'Well, yes,' Diane admitted, retreating slightly from the other girl's obvious anger. 'He said you'd found something else that you would be starting right away— that he was letting you leave without having to work out your notice.'

'That was big of him!' Charlotte charged sarcastically, turning to glare at the schedule. The bastard, the double-crossing *bastard*!

'Well, don't you have something else lined up?' the secretary asked tentatively.

'No, I don't!'

'Perhaps it was a misunderstanding, then,' Diane placated, looking decidedly uncomfortable.

Realising how unfair it was to take her anger with Harris out on the other girl, she nodded. 'Yes, maybe it was a misunderstanding,' she prevaricated grimly. 'Where can I find Mr Jordan?'

'He's left the office already.' The secretary pulled her appointments book to her and opened it. 'He doesn't have a meeting, so if he's still in the building he's probably up in his suite.' She looked up at Charlotte. 'It's the penthouse on the top floor. Would you like me to ring up and see if he's there? I'll ask if he has time to see you?' she offered helpfully.

Charlotte hesitated, then shook her head. 'I'll. . .I'll see him in the morning,' she lied. After what he'd done, he just might be too big a rat to face her. She had every intention of settling this tonight  and he wasn't going to get any warning.

Dredging up a smile for the secretary, Charlotte left the office. Outside in the hall, she turned towards the lifts with a determined stride.

# CHAPTER FIVE

IF CHARLOTTE had been a comic-strip character, her creator would have drawn little puffs of steam coming out of her ears when she stepped out of the lift a few minutes later. Her temper had escalated with the rising lift and she couldn't remember ever being so angry— no, mad, she was damn mad. Harris had no right to fire her. She was a good worker, doing her job with skill and willingness. Just because his prissy fiancée might disapprove of his past indiscretions, it didn't give him the right to sweep her under the rug like a piece of dirt!

There was only one door leading off the square hallway that she found herself in. Striding over to it, she hammered on the sturdy walnut panels and, when it didn't open immediately, tried the doorknob. It gave beneath her fingers, so she twisted it and pushed the door open. Storming through the portal, she sent the door slamming behind her with a resounding crash and marched forward into—an empty room.

Her chest heaving as if she had actually climbed the stairs to this penthouse eyrie, she surveyed the luxurious sitting-room, seeking an occupant. Deep-pile carpeting lay beneath her feet, pale grey suede covered the walls. Two enormous black leather sofas dominated the scene, flanked by modernistic glass side-tables. The far wall, consisting entirely of floor-to-ceiling windows, was curved to form a quarter-circle, affording an unimpeded view of the city and mountains.

The room, however, contained no people. Feeling a little like an actress who'd made her grand entrance only to find the theatre empty, Charlotte glared balefully at the Chinese vase that she had no opportunity to throw at its owner.

A sudden noise behind her sent her spinning around. 'What the. . .hell are you doing here?' Harris spluttered, coming into the room from the side hall. His hair was damp, drops of water rolling off it to splatter down his bared chest. He'd flung a back-towel around his middle and, as he stared at his unexpected guest, he pulled it tighter to secure it.

Dry-mouthed, Charlotte stared back at him. Her rage had faltered with the anticlimax of not finding him immediately. Confronted suddenly by his virtually nude body dealt it a near-fatal blow. Charlotte couldn't take her eyes from him, thoughts and desires she had no right to entertain swamping her consciousness. His chest was deeply tanned, heavily muscled beneath its mat of curling hair. His belly was hard and flat above the towel slung low on his hips. Feeling slightly giddy, Charlotte pulled her gaze from her contemplation of the towel and met his eyes.

'Well, if you've seen enough, maybe you wouldn't mind telling what the hell you're doing barging in here,' Harris growled sarcastically.

Her face scorching, aware that he had read her thoughts, Charlotte looked down at her hands and tried to remember just why she had come to see him. Memory returned swiftly—and with it anger.

She lambasted him with her opinion, scathing if somewhat disjointed. 'I came to tell you that I think you're a low-down, conniving *worm*. I don't know where you come off going around like some tin-god Hitler, but I think you stink. You *said* I could keep my job and no sooner do I turn my back than you've fired me. It would serve you right if I told your precious fiancée just what kind of skunk. . .you are!'

She ran out of steam—or maybe she was arrested by the look on his face. He was pale, his jaw a hard line, working with anger. He didn't move, but stared at her with an icy menace that was infinitely chilling. Charlotte found her anger once again waning, this time supplanted by fear. She had blithely rushed in here, intent on venting her rage, unheeding of the consequences. Perhaps she had thought he would be cowed; instead, he was like a coiled rattler ready to strike, dangerous and deadly.

'Are you trying to blackmail me?' he asked in a low, ominous voice.

'Not blackmail. I didn't mean that,' Charlotte backed off hastily, none the less shamed by the acknowledgment that he frightened her.

'What *did* you mean, then?' he enquired, still stern, but not quite so forbidding.

'I meant. . .' The towel had slipped a bit, riding down on his hips and exposing the lighter skin his bathing trunks had covered. She couldn't meet his eyes—they were too intimidating. However, the view lower down was dauntingly distracting.

'I meant. . .' She *forced* her eyes up to his face. Made impatient by her stammering, Harris moved slightly, and at the edge of her vision Charlotte saw the towel inch down another fraction. The words dried once more in her throat as unconsciously she held her breath, her gaze drawn relentlessly to the insecure covering.

'For God's sake, can't you get on with it?' Harris demanded, shrugging with exasperation and further imperilling the wrap.

'Sorry,' she muttered. 'I. . .' She shook her head, then returned his look of exasperation. 'Could you please go get dressed?' she demanded, her face going red.

His eyebrows shot up in surprise, then he glanced downwards. He caught the edge of the towel just as the end he'd tucked in at his waist slipped free. His fingers clasping the top edge of the wrap to hold it up, he looked over at her, taking in her crimson cheeks and flustered expression.

'You could have called and made an appointment to see me,' he advised her harshly. 'As it happened, I wasn't expecting company.'

Reduced to training her eyes on the rug, she stammered, 'I—I know, I just. . .didn't think.' She brought her eyes up to his, pleading, 'You could get dressed now. I'll wait.'

'Gee, thanks,' he drawled sarcastically. He held her eyes steadily for a moment, a light of malacious laughter overlaying the angry glint. 'However, since you were so anxious to see me, I'll not make you wait.' He looked down to adjust the towel, and for a moment she was afraid he was going to discard it altogether. He could be just that nasty. However, he finally secured it, and when he looked up again his face wore a vindictive grin.

'Don't worry, I'm not cold. I just turned the air-conditioning on when I came in a few minutes ago. It hasn't had time to cool the place off yet.' He eyed her mockingly. 'As a matter of fact, you're looking a bit warm,' he taunted with false concern. 'Maybe you should take off your jacket.'

Warm! She felt as if she were on fire! It wasn't just embarrassment, either! Harris was an extremely attractive man, very virile, very masculine—and Charlotte wasn't a nun! She'd lain with this man, spent one entire night exploring the secrets of that lean, hard body. Even if it had been years ago, the memory was still fresh and clear. She knew the contours of his hips and thighs, the tiny scar along his left rib, the warm feel of his skin against hers. How could she ever forget?

Speechless, Charlotte stood imprisoned by unwanted desire, helpless and humiliated. Her body, her heart, insisted that this man belonged to her, and telling herself he was Janice's, that he didn't belong to her any more, didn't seem to do any good. She was honest and moral; she didn't poach on other women's preserves. And yet. . .

A taunting smile playing about his lips, Harris sauntered over to her, stopping a few inches in front of her. She caught the drifting scent of soap, the damp warmth of his skin.

'I'll help you take it off,' he tormented, lifting his hands to her shoulders and slipping them beneath the lapels of her jacket. Beneath it, she wore a sleeveless

top made of a silky synthetic fabric, and his fingers
burned through the material.

Only by keeping herself rigid, every muscle tensed,
could she keep rein on the rampant emotions driving
through her. He knew he affected her, but, strugging
with her pride, she couldn't allow him to see just how
much. It would be all too mortifying to melt all over
him like an ice-cream cone in the sun.

Slowly, sadistically, he eased the jacket off her
shoulders, his touch caressing, his gaze riveted to her
face. It was a cruel torture, and her nerves quivered
with tension.

The jacket had only reached the tops of her arms
when he glanced down, and suddenly his expression
changed. Following his gaze, Charlotte looked downwards, biting her lip as she realised her betrayal. The
blouse she wore was finely woven, the material like
gossamer. She'd worn it job-hunting, wanting to look
her best. The fine, insubstantial material clung to her
breasts, though, clearly revealing the hard, aroused
nubs of her nipples.

Harris's fingers tightened against her shoulders and
she swiftly found his eyes. Amusement, anger—they
had fled, burned out by the passion that flamed in their
silvery depths.

'Harris?' she whispered. Her control unravelling, she
raised her hand to touch his chest. His skin was warm,
still faintly damp from his shower, and beneath it she
could feel the heavy beat of his heart.

'Charlotte, I. . .' Suddenly, he roughly pulled her
jacket back up on to her shoulders, shattering the
moment of intimacy. Stepping back, he half turned

away from her, raking his fingers through the dark pelt of his hair. She saw that his hand was trembling slightly. When he turned his head to look back at her, his expression was bitter and condemning. 'You were right. I'll go get dressed—then we can talk.' Swinging on his heel, he stalked out of the room.

Alone, Charlotte stood where she was for several seconds. She glanced to the door, wishing she had never come here, wishing she could leave. They had to get this settled, though. She needed her job. Finally, she walked to one of the sofas and subsided on to it. The smooth leather felt chill against her heated skin.

When Harris returned several minutes later he was fully and formally dressed. His dark grey business suit was well cut and sombre, his crisp white shirt immaculate. He looked cool, remote and very much in charge.

'Would you care for a drink?' he asked politely, moving over to a cabinet situated against the far wall.

'I. . .' Charlotte hesitated, clearing her throat. She had been unable to whip up her previous feeling of anger while he was dressing, and without it to sustain her she found her nerves twitching. Probably she should keep a clear head, but the idea of some alcohol to steady her, although she seldom drank, appealed greatly. 'Yes, please. I'll. . .er. . .have a pink squirrel. . .' *How* could she possibly have come out with that? At his look of dry enquiry, she hastily stammered an amendment. 'I mean, a glass of wine. White wine, if you have it.'

'I do.' Harris turned to the cabinet and busied himself preparing the drinks. Staring at his broad back, Charlotte strove to get a grip on herself. She felt only slightly more composed when he turned back and brought her the drink.

Gripping the cool, long-stemmed glass in tight fingers, she tentatively took a sip as Harris settled himself on the sofa opposite hers.

'Now, what seems to be the problem?' he asked, having sampled his own drink. His glass held straight whisky over ice, yet with his appearance of ease and relaxation he didn't seem to need its restorative powers, Charlotte thought resentfully.

'The problem is that you fired me!' she answered, feeling the heat of anger returning. 'On Friday night you told me I could keep my job, but when I came in this afternoon Diane told me you'd taken me off the schedule.'

Casually, Harris held up his glass, inspecting its contents before taking another sip. Lowering the glass, he reminded her, 'As I recall, you told me you'd be looking for another job.'

'I know. . .that's what I've been doing all day. There isn't anything out there.' Oh, she was back in her stride now, adrenalin bubbling through her veins as her resentment flourished. 'I need to work—and I need this job at the Black Stallion because it's the only one I can get.'

Smiling, he met the angry gleam in her eye with equanimity. 'No, it isn't,' he informed her smugly. 'I've found you another one.'

Charlotte eyed him suspiciously. 'Doing what?' She could just imagine—digging ditches, or maybe on a dust-cart!

'Working in a hotel—not as a waitress, though. A friend of mine has an opening for a receptionist.'

That didn't sound so bad—the work would be less demanding than waitressing, and she wouldn't have to wear a skimpy uniform. For some reason, though, she still felt uneasy. 'I could start immediately?'

'As soon as you're able,' he answered. 'It's really quite an opportunity. There's no future in being a cocktail waitress—it's a dead-end job. Working for Steve. . .who knows?' He shrugged. 'You could work your way into management eventually. You're a bright girl.'

'Thanks,' Charlotte said drily, resenting his condescension. 'And no, thanks. I don't need a permanent job just now. I have another job lined up for the fall—teaching grade one at an elementary school. Maybe you figure that's a dead-end job as well, but I'm looking forward to it.'

'You earned your degree?' He had the grace to look duly impressed, if unflatteringly surprised.

'That's right. . .just this spring.' He sent her an approving look and she couldn't resist adding, 'I was eighth in my class.'

'Very impressive. Did your father help you out?'

'I haven't seen my father for over five years,' Charlotte said shortly. 'I paid my own way through school. . .and I still need a job—the one I had until you fired me,' she finished pointedly.

Harris regarded her silently for a moment, then said, 'I think that if I talked to Steve, explained the circumstances, he'd let you have the receptionist's job just for the summer.'

Not wanting to capitulate too hastily, she asked cautiously, 'How much does it pay?'

He named a figure that was well above what she had been making as a waitress. Her eyebrows lifted, her interest truly caught, and he continued, 'Of course, you'd still have to work most weekends, but you're used to that. It is a day job, though.'

'That wouldn't be a problem,' she allowed, unwittingly showing her interest. Working days would solve a problem, not create one. She wasn't happy about leaving Jimmy alone at night. She worried about him in the dark hours, at home by himself without anyone to call on if he needed help. During the day, he still managed to get out once in a while, going for walks in the park, making his way down to the Elks for a game of cribbage.

'I think you'd find the Westerly a pleasant place to work,' Harris carried on, pressing his advantage. 'It isn't as large as the Foothills; it's older, elegant, but somehow homey, if you know what I mean.'

'That sounds perfect,' Charlotte admitted. She didn't recognise the name of the hotel, but that didn't matter. The Foothills had always seemed too big, too modern for her tastes. Suddenly she smiled at her former boss. Maybe Harris wasn't such a scoundrel after all. He seemed to have really looked for something that would suit her. 'You said that I could start right away?'

'As soon as you've settled. I forgot to tell you, you'll be expected to live in.'

'Live in?' she frowned. 'But I have an apartment. I don't——'

'Your present place is a little far away for commuting,' he interrupted her smoothly.

'What do you mean?'

'The Westerly is in Seattle. . .but, as I said, accommodation is included—*single* accommodation,' he reiterated meaningfully.

'Single. . .?' She caught her breath as his motive became clear. She'd been right to be suspicious of his offer. 'In other words, Jimmy wouldn't be welcome!'

'I'm afraid not.'

Smoothing down the front of her skirt, Charlotte got deliberately to her feet. 'Then I think you ought to be able to guess where you can put your friend Steve's job.'

Before she could walk out, Harris was at her side, staying her with his hand on her arm. She glared down at it, but he didn't release her. 'Don't be hasty, Charlotte!' he advised. 'Think it over. This offer might be just the opportunity you need to get out of an untenable situation.'

'What do you know about my "situation"?' she demanded, jerking her arm away so he had to release her.

'Quite a bit, actually. I had a talk with the bartender the other night——'

'I heard about that,' Charlotte cut him off. 'What right have you to question my friends, go snooping into my affairs?'

Harris looked faintly uncomfortable. 'I was curious and then, well. . .I'm concerned about you, as I would be about any old friend who I heard was in something of a mess.'

'The mess meaning Jimmy?' She sent him a look of disdain.

He returned it with an implacable look of his own. 'Yes, to be blunt, Jimmy, this fellow you're living with. Tony tells me he doesn't even have a job—obviously he leeches off you. And I heard the way he talked to you on the phone the other night! He ought to be horsewhipped!' Harris expostulated, clenching his fist and slamming it into his open palm.

Charlotte was taken aback by his vehemence, her own anger subsiding. She felt a little guilty about her deception of Harris. If he knew all the facts, that Jimmy was in fact eighty-five years old and a victim of Alzheimer's disease, that whole phone conversation would have sounded different. She couldn't bring herself to tell him though, but did allow, 'I don't support Jimmy. He has. . .' she hesitated, not wanting to say pension, so substituted '. . .an income.'

'He has an income. . .' Harris scathed. 'And yet here you are begging to keep your job hustling drinks in that dive downstairs! Why won't that bum support you if you're living together?'

Charlotte skittered a look at his furious face. What was Harris so mad about? Even if things were the way he thought they were, surely his reaction exceeded the bounds of simple concern for an old friend? Unbidden, a tiny tremor of delight ran down her spine. What if Harris really was concerned for her, still cared? What if he were jealous of Jimmy?

'I. . .er. . .Jimmy doesn't get that much each month,' Charlotte explained, stalling while she considered the idea. Surreptitiously, she slid him a glance, sliding it on by when his gaze sought to connect with hers. She looked past him at a section of the room that had been out of view when she had been seated on the divan. That must be why she hadn't noticed the photograph before. It was of Janice and Harris, capturing them for all time in a casual, loving pose, their arms intertwined as they laughed at some private joke.

The joke was on her, though, she thought, ruthlessly squelching that flicker of hope she'd nurtured. Her eyes met Harris's. 'I hadn't realised you were such a busybody, Harris. Why don't you just tend to your own business and I'll tend to mine?' she suggested icily. 'As for my dead-end job in your "dive", well, it's the only damn one I seem to be able to find in this town, so for now I'd like to have it back.'

'You won't even consider Steve's offer?'

'No—even if you won't let me work here.' He glared at her with contempt and she thrust her chin out in a defiant angle. He'd been right—she'd *begged* for her job back, but she'd had enough. Somehow, she'd manage without it.

Gathering her dignity about her like a cloak, she stepped around him and moved towards the door. She'd reached it, and her hand was on the knob, when he said flatly, 'Call Diane tomorrow afternoon. I'll tell her in the morning to put you back on the schedule.'

Surprised, Charlotte turned to look at him. His face was hard and unapproachable. None the less, she stammered, 'I. . .er. . .thank you.'

He shrugged off her gratitude. 'If letting drunks paw you night after night and then going home to some guy who treats you like dirt is what you want, then don't let me interfere. I shouldn't have wasted my time trying to help you out in the first place.' Dismissing her, he turned and picked up the glass he'd been drinking from earlier. The ice had melted, diluting the amber whisky to pale gold. None the less, he raised it to his lips and drained the glass. As he moved towards the cocktail cabinet, Charlotte slipped out of the door.

# CHAPTER SIX

CHARLOTTE wrinkled her nose at the odour of paint, sawdust and new carpeting that assailed her when she stepped into the lounge to start her evening shift. The Black Stallion was almost unrecognisable these days. Bright sunlight streamed in through the windows that had been installed to overlook the hotel pool, dissipating the dimly lit cave-like atmosphere that had once distinguished the bar.

It wasn't the physical changes that Harris had ordered that gave the lounge such a different feeling, though. A new clientele had started to frequent the tavern. The older, beer-drinking, predominantly male crowd that previously patronised the Black Stallion were being edged out by a younger, more sophisticated crowd. More couples came in now, and even unescorted women stopped by for a quiet drink. The country and western records on the juke-box had been replaced with soft rock tunes and they filtered through the air as the newcomers made small talk over their white wine and Perrier.

About the only flaw in the Black Stallion's 'new look' was that Charlotte felt even more self-conscious wearing her old skimpy uniform than she ever had before. At least in the 'old' Black Stallion's somewhat tacky atmosphere the scantiness of her attire hadn't seemed too out of place. However, amid the bright sunlight and well-dressed women patrons Charlotte felt like an exhibitionist.

Of course, Harris was changing the uniforms to match the lounge's new uptown image. They had already been ordered, but some hold-up at the factory had delayed their delivery. And until they arrived the waitresses had to make do with the ones they had.

Consequently, Charlotte was somewhat surprised to find Linda wearing one of the new uniforms when she reached the bar. 'Where did you get that?' Charlotte demanded, enviously eyeing her co-worker's apparel. The straight denim skirt and waistcoat with yellow gingham shirt were a vast improvement over the 'dance-hall' costume. Not only were they neat, attractive *and* unrevealing, but eminently practical as well. Any stains and spills collected through a night's work of passing out drinks would hardly show on the dark blue material of the skirt, and would easily come out in the wash. Letting her gaze drift downwards, Charlotte knew that the white high-topped moccasins would be just the ticket for feet that rebelled at being jammed into spike heels every night.

'They handed out the new uniforms at the meeting this morning,' Linda informed her. 'You didn't go,' she added in critical accusation.

Charlotte didn't bother replying. Harris had arranged several employee/management meetings since he had taken over, but she hadn't attended any of them. The rest of his employees, even Tony, seemed really to enjoy going to them and feeling that they were having a part in the decision-making process at the hotel. She might have gone herself, but. . . She sighed.

How could she, when Harris was so obviously avoiding her? He might think she was pushing herself at him if he saw her at one of his meetings, was using it as an excuse just to be in the same room with him.

The trouble was, she wasn't sure that wouldn't be her reason for going. Harris hadn't been in the bar when she was there since the afternoon she'd gone to see him in his apartment. She should have been relieved—but instead, as the weeks passed, she found herself longing for the sight of him. She knew there could never be anything between them again, but knowing he was so close and yet so remote was a fine torture on her nerves.

To her surprise, though, she did see him that night. She had just gone up to a table of two men to take their orders when from the corner of her eyes she saw Harris enter the lounge through the lobby door. He didn't sit at a table, but walked up to the bar to speak with Tony.

Her first impulse was to abandon her customers and follow him—just to be close to him, to hear his voice again. When she'd left his apartment that afternoon, she had wished she'd never have to encounter him again, but time had cured that notion.

However, a sense of duty and an attack of cold feet kept her at the table. Giving the men a welcoming smile, she asked for their order.

Instead of answering her, the younger peered up into her face. 'I know you, don't I?' he asked.

Charlotte maintained her smile, saying, 'I don't think so.' *That* line was as old as the hills! Her pencil poised over her pad, she asked again, 'And what would you like to drink this evening?'

The other man ordered beer for the two of them, while his friend continued to subject her to a searching appraisal. Embarrassment prickled the back of Charlotte's neck, all Harris's scornful words about the unsavoury characters that she had to deal with in her work coming to the fore. Why couldn't he have just continued to stay out of the lounge when she was working? she asked herself contradictorily as she half turned and saw him watching her.

Before she could leave the table, though, her customer caught her arm, exclaiming, 'I've got it! You're Charlie, Charlie Harper. We went to school together at Platte Valley High.'

Swinging back to the table, Charlotte stared at him in astonishment. It had been so long since she'd run into anyone from those days when she'd lived with her father that she had almost forgotten that that had been part of her life once. Now she thought about it, though, he did look familiar. 'I'm sorry, I can't recall your name.'

'Gary, Gary Sanders. I sat beside you in maths class.'

'Oh, I remember now,' Charlotte admitted, wondering why she'd failed to recognise him at first. He looked much the same, only older and perhaps a bit better-looking. He'd been the heart-throb of Mr Martin's algebra class—he'd also invariably tried to copy the answers from her paper when they had had a test! 'Well, it's nice to see you again,' Charlotte said conventionally, not really meaning it. She'd been one of the few girls unimpressed by Gary's corn-blond hair and football-player physique.

Before she could take her leave, though, Gary said quickly, 'I never expected to find you working in a place like this—you were always such a stick-in-the-mud! We've got to get together and catch up on old times.' Charlotte smiled non-committally, then he went on enthusiastically, 'Look, if you're not busy tomorrow night, there's this party. . .?'

She didn't have a chance to form her refusal before a deep male—familiar—voice said from behind her, 'Is there some problem here, Charlie?'

Her nerves rioting at Harris's unexpected arrival, she jerked around. 'No, of course, not Har——' the look in his cold, steely eyes caused her to amend hastily '—Mr Jordan.' He'd turned his attention to her customers, eyeing them with barely concealed animosity. Feeling compelled to offer some explanation as to why she lingered at their table, although it hadn't been *that* long, Charlotte stammered, 'Gary. . .Gary and I went to high school together.'

'Really,' Harris commented grimly, then looked at her and sent a shiver of apprehension down her spine. 'Well, I suggest you save your reminiscing for your own time. That party over by the door has been trying to get your attention for quite a while.'

Blushing fiery red at the reprimand handed out in front of the other men, Charlotte glanced over to the table he'd indicated. The couple were obviously engrossed in one another and could probably not care less about when she took their drinks order. Her lips flattened in an indignant line, she looked back at her employer.

She glared at him, but didn't dare say anything. He was just looking for an excuse to fire her. She could tell by the look on his face that nothing would delight him more. Finally, she forced herself to move away.

She'd only gone a couple of paces when Gary called out to her, 'Hey, what about the party?'

Charlotte hesitated, glancing first at him then at Harris. She could see anger smouldering in her ex-fiancé's eyes. She looked back at Gary, forcing a warm smile to her lips. 'Sure, sounds like fun. You can call me at home tomorrow to set up the time—I'm in the book.' Flashing Harris's stony countenance a triumphant look, she started to stalk away.

Harris's hand on her arm seared like a firebrand as he held her back. For several seconds, his granite eyes raked her form before clashing with her violet eyes. 'I hate to be the one to cramp your style, sweetheart, but the reason I came in tonight was to make sure you had one of the new uniforms. As soon as you've finished serving these two tables, I want you to go and change into it.' Once again sliding his eyes scornfully down her scantily clad body, he advised, 'I'm afraid if you intend to keep on working for me you're going to have to start displaying your merchandise just a little less blatantly.'

Feeling as though he had slapped her, she watched him walk from the lounge.

Idly, Charlotte let her eyes drift over the crowded shed, searching out her escort. There must have been two hundred people attending the party held in Gary's

employers' new machinery shed—and all seemed to be
having a whale of a time, herself included. The evening
had been great fun. Since her break with her father,
Charlotte had lived the life of a city girl. She'd forgotten the good things about rural life, the friendliness
and hospitality. The guests at the party, invited to
inaugurate the new building on the Mitchell ranch, had
been without exception cordial and welcoming to her.

Even Gary hadn't turned out too badly, even if she
had only agreed to go out with him to annoy Harris.
While she still wasn't exactly enamoured of him, he'd
proved to be a courteous and undemanding escort so
far. He'd introduced her around when they'd first
arrived, and danced with her a few times before they'd
been separated. However, as she didn't particularly
want him sticking to her like glue all evening, she
hadn't felt abandoned. There had been plenty of other
people to keep her entertained, so she hadn't really
missed his company.

Espying him now at the far side of the room, she
eased her way through the crowd. While all in all it
had been a good evening, unfortunately it was going to
have to end soon. It was gone midnight and, while she
was used to late nights from her job, she was none the
less tired—deliciously tired. Getting away from
Boulder and the Foothills, away from the danger of
bumping into Harris or his fiancée, had been just what
she needed. She felt more relaxed than she had in
weeks. Maybe tonight she would be able to get a good
night's sleep for a change.

Gary was sitting on one of the benches that ringed
the shed, his long jean-clad legs stretched out in front

of him, his back against the wall. He'd removed the string tie he'd worn earlier and opened the collar of his western shirt. He looked totally relaxed as he sipped beer from a paper cup and watched the milling crowd.

When Charlotte walked up to him, he looked up and gave her a crooked smile, his eyes overbright, his face slightly flushed. 'Hi, beautiful, I was wondering what you'd been up to.' He reached up and pulled her down beside him. Before Charlotte could react, he'd planted a boozy kiss on her lips.

No need for her to wonder what *he* had been up to! She gave him a chastening frown. While she'd been dancing, talking, enjoying the company—he'd been enjoying the beer keg.

She supposed it would be too much to hope that he would relinquish the car keys to her. He just didn't strike her as the type to admit that he'd had too much to drink. The only alternative would be to try to sober him up. 'I thought I'd find you so that we could get some dessert and coffee?' she suggested brightly.

Judging from the look on his face, she might as well have suggested they share bat-wings laced with arsenic. 'I'm not hungry,' he said, taking another slurp of beer. 'You go ahead, though.'

'Well, I guess I'm not that hungry either,' Charlotte said, disgruntled. The music pulsed around them as Gary sat steadily draining his glass of beer, and Charlotte wondered what she was going to do now. When her escort tipped the paper cup to get the last drop from it and started getting to his feet to fetch a refill, she knew she had to think of something.

'Let's dance.' She jumped up before he could move

off towards the beer keg. 'You've hardly danced with me at all tonight.' She gave him a winning smile—he couldn't drink while they were dancing.

He stared at her blearily for a moment, then shrugged. 'Sure, why not?' He tossed the empty cup aside and, taking her by the arm, towed her over to the section of floor where other couples were gyrating to the music. To Charlotte's delight, the band was playing a lively pop tune—strenuous exercise should help sober Gary up. However, he had other ideas. Ignoring the tempo, he pulled her into a clinch and began slowly shuffling around the floor.

For a minute she thought he might crack her ribs, and she wriggled uneasily in his embrace. Fortunately, he loosened his hold slightly in response, although he was still leaning heavily against her. His breath was hot and beery against her neck and she felt her face heat up as he pressed against her, his arousal evident.

His tongue came out to caress the lobe of her ear and a shiver of distaste coursed down her spine. She tried struggling away from him, but because she didn't want to draw too much attention to them her efforts were ineffectual.

He whispered in her ear, 'I couldn't believe my luck when I saw you in the bar last night. You've sure changed from the scrawny kid I knew at school.' He chuckled, doing a quick turn in response to the music and staggering slightly. Charlotte sagged under his weight as she kept him upright.

'Yup,' he continued, 'I couldn't believe my luck.' Charlotte couldn't believe hers, either! All bad! Although she supposed it was her own fault. Talk about cutting your nose off to spite your face! How had she let animosity towards Harris goad her into going out with this turkey? 'I like that sexy outfit you work in—although you look good in these tight jeans too.' Fitting action to words, he slid his hand down her back to cup her bottom through the denim.

Charlotte jerked in his arms as though he'd bit her. He eased his hold and looked into her face, frowning slightly. Quickly, she said, 'Why don't we sit down? I'm tired of dancing.' Even sitting around watching him get soused was better than this! Maybe if he had enough he'd pass out, then she could drive herself home.

'Sure, if you say so,' he agreed easily enough. As he turned to lead her from the floor, his arm clamped possessively about her shoulders, he asked, 'Would you rather just split? Get out of here?'

Charlotte slid him an assessing glance. She was dying to leave, to be back at her apartment, safe and able to put Gary Sanders right out of her mind. Even if he had ideas of coming in with her—Jimmy might be old, but he made a darn good chaperon! She wished Gary hadn't had quite so much to drink before driving, but. . .

'Sure. Let's leave. I'd just like to say goodbye to the Mitchells and thank them for having me.'

'Whatever you say,' he agreed nonchalantly, steering her towards the older couple standing near the entrance. They were talking to another couple and it wasn't until she'd almost reached them that Charlotte realised who they were. *Damn*! Was it only malicious fate that had brought Harris and his fiancée here tonight, or had he somehow found out that this was where Gary was taking her?

Gary spoke up, giving her a moment to gather her composure. 'I'll guess we'll be heading out, boss. Great party.'

Mr Mitchell gave the younger man an appraising look. 'You looked as if you were having a good time,' he said drily, taking in the young man's flushed face and overbright eyes.

Charlotte found her voice. 'Yes, we did. I had a lovely time and thank you for having me.' She held out her hand to the older couple and, when they'd shaken it, let it drop back to her side. Maybe if she just pretended Harris and Janice weren't even there she could handle the humiliation of their seeing her with this drunk.

'I'm glad you came,' Mrs Mitchell assured her. 'It was nice meeting you.'

Before they could move on, Mr Mitchell intervened. He'd been giving his employee some hard looks, and now he said, 'It looks as if you've had a few. It might be wise to let someone else drive your date home.'

Gary was ruffled. 'Heck, I'm OK. It takes more than a few beers to bother me.' He looked at Charlotte for support, his arm crushing her shoulders. As she looked up at him uncertainly, his lips slid wetly over her cheekbone. 'I'm fine. . .ain't that right, honey?' His hand slid down around her waist and, snaking under her arm, it fingered the underside of her breast. Charlotte flinched.

'I can run Charlie back into town.' Harris's offer fell

into the embarrassed silence that followed Gary's action.

'But, Harry, darling, we just got here,' Janice protested, hanging on to his arm and pouting up at him. He looked down into his fiancée's face with a gentle expression on his own.

'It won't take more than a few minutes,' he assured her. Treating Gary to a frosty look, he added grimly, 'I think I *should* escort Charlotte home.'

Janice still looked sulky when Charlotte hastily intervened, 'I'm sure Gary's fine. I don't mind his taking me home.' That was a bald lie, but given the alternative. . .the ride back into town might be uncomfortable, even hazardous with Gary driving her, but not nearly as uncomfortable and hazardous as it would be with Harris at the wheel.

Gary rewarded her for her support by swinging her to him and clamping his mouth over hers in a hard, probing kiss. 'That's my girl!' he applauded when he finally released her. Charlotte felt a little sick—worse when she caught Harris's and Janice's expressions. His would have formed an icecap at the equator, while Janice's merely reflected all the disgust she herself was feeling.

However, she was stuck with Gary now. Striving for some semblance of dignity, she followed him out through the exit.

Charlotte's head was throbbing by the time they were on their way. There had been a brief altercation getting into the car. Gary had expected her to sit in the middle of the bench seat cuddled up to him as he drove, and she'd flatly refused. Even if she had felt inclined towards Gary—which she didn't—in his condition, he didn't need any distractions from the road. Besides, while it was undoubtedly stupid to let a drunk drive her anywhere, it would be doubly so not to put on a seatbelt.

Once they were under way, she was relieved to find that Gary seemed content to maintain a sedate speed, and after a few minutes she relaxed enough to close her eyes. They hadn't gone much further, though, when she felt the car turn, then lurch as it moved over an uneven roadbed. Her eyes flew open and she saw several bales of hay bordering the lane, then Gary braked and killed the headlights.

In disbelief, she turned her head to stare at her escort in the pale moonlight. He couldn't possibly be so juvenile as to think she would enjoy stopping in a deserted field to do a spot of necking, could he? She'd expected she might have a bit of trouble with him when they got back to her apartment, but she knew Jimmy would take care of that. It was beginning to look unfortunate that he wasn't with them for the ride home.

Gary had quickly unhooked his seatbelt and now slid across the seat to her side. Before she could evade him, he claimed her mouth in a long, wet kiss. Confined by her own seatbelt and his arms, Charlotte struggled for air. Finally she got her hand under his chin and was able to push his face away. 'You've got to be kidding!' she exploded.

'What do you mean?' Gary asked obtusely, nuzzling her neck.

Deftly, Charlotte untangled his arms from about her

# UP TO 6 FREE GIFTS FOR YOU!
## Look inside—all gifts are absolutely free!

NO POSTAGE
NECESSARY
IF MAILED
IN THE
UNITED STATES

# BUSINESS REPLY MAIL
FIRST CLASS MAIL    PERMIT NO. 717    BUFFALO, NY

POSTAGE WILL BE PAID BY ADDRESSEE

## HARLEQUIN READER SERVICE
3010 WALDEN AVE
PO BOX 1867
BUFFALO NY 14240-9952

# Behind These Doors!

# GIFTS

---

## SEE WHAT'S FREE!

**FREE** TWO HARLEQUIN BOOKS. Yours for the asking.

**FREE** BONUS GIFT! Victorian Picture Frame

**FREE** TWO MORE HARLEQUIN BOOKS.

**FREE** MYSTERY GIFT!

In addition to everything else!

Open all four doors to find out what gifts are yours for the asking from the Harlequin Reader Service.®

Just peel off the four "door" stickers.

**YES!** I have removed all four stickers. Please send me the free gifts revealed beneath the doors. I understand that under the terms explained on the facing page no purchase is necessary and I may cancel at any time.

NAME

(PLEASE PRINT)

ADDRESS                                                                 APT.

CITY

STATE                          ZIP CODE

106 CIH ACK9
(U-H-P-07/91)

# PEEK-A-BOO!

# Free Gifts For You!

*Look inside—Right Now!*
*We've got something*
*special just for you!*

(U-H-P-07/91)

shoulders and, pushing him away, she glared at him. He looked back at her with what appeared to be genuine puzzlement. 'You can't honestly think I'm going to put up with being mauled in some car! I thought I'd left those kind of wrestling matches back in high school,' she advised him scornfully.

'You don't like making love in a car?' he asked.

'What do you think?' she demanded, reaching down to adjust her blouse where his pawing had wrenched it askew. She didn't see him reach down beside her, but suddenly the back of her seat fell away from her.

'Then you've never been in a car like mine,' he informed her as she stared up into his face in bewilderment. 'It's just like a double bed in here!' He leaned over to switch on the radio and, as music flooded the car, reached over to unhook her seatbelt. Hauling her with him, he moved back until they were supine on the 'bed'. 'Isn't this cosy?' he asked, trapping her with his arm across her midriff as he sought the creamy flesh of her neck with his lips.

Charlotte punched him in the shoulder with her fist and he jerked himself upwards to stare down into her face in blank astonishment. For a moment, she almost felt sorry for him—it must be a real handicap to be so stupid! However, pity didn't temper her anger much. 'You conceited baboon! I wouldn't make love with you if you provided me with satin sheets and a feather bed! You turn my stomach. Now put this seat up and take me home!' she ordered.

As she struggled to sit up, his hands came down on her shoulders, pinning her against the makeshift bed. His pale blue eyes glittered down at her furiously and, trapped by his superior strength, she felt a tremor of fear course through her. 'Now, aren't you the hoity-toity one? Come off it, babe. I know what kind of chicks work in bars. You're nothing but a cheap whore, and I'll be having what you let everybody else have!'

Impotent rage filled her as he lowered his head to kiss her again. She didn't deserve this. She worked hard at her job, earning her living the best way she could. She had never been promiscuous and few of the waitresses that worked at the Black Stallion were. It was so unfair, she railed inwardly, twisting her head to evade his mouth.

His hands moved to the side of her head to hold it steady and he kissed her lingeringly. He'd moved his body to lie on top of her and she was crushed beneath his weight, unable to struggle. After an interminable time, he finally raised his head. 'Now wasn't that nice?' he asked softly, smiling down at her as he stroked the fine wisps of hair back from her forehead.

Charlotte felt like vomiting, but fear kept her silent. Anger had got her nowhere. Gary seemed to have regained his temper, but her shoulders still felt bruised from where he'd held her down. Instinct warned that to vent the rage and frustration she was feeling would only make things worse.

She swallowed hard. 'That. . .that was nice,' she croaked.

'I knew you were just playing hard to get,' Gary murmured complacently. His finger toyed with the top button of her blouse, then slid it through the hole. 'You have lovely skin—so soft and smooth.' He touched his lips to the ridge of her collarbone.

Charlotte shifted uneasily beneath him, her skin crawling away from his touch. He looked up. 'I'm too heavy?' His hand rested on her breast.

She saw an opening and dived through it. 'Er. . .you are a bit,' she agreed, forcing a giggle. 'I'm feeling a little squashed.'

'OK.' As he shifted to the side of her, Charlotte scooted away from him. Keeping her eyes riveted on Gary and trying to look congenial, she felt along the door for the handle. As her hand closed over the cold metal lever, Gary leaned over her, undoing another button on her shirt. 'You have nice tits, too,' he complimented crudely, slipping his fingers beneath her lacy bra in search of her nipple.

'Gee. . .thanks,' Charlotte said. As he touched the tip of her breast, she cringed. 'Don't!' He lifted his head, eyeing her suspiciously. She tried to smile, improvising. 'Don't you think we could have a window open? It's getting hot in here.'

'Only because we have too many clothes on,' he teased, and her heart sank. She was hanging on to the door-handle like a lifeline, but she didn't dare open it yet. He was still too close to her, still half lying on her. If she tried to escape and failed, there was no telling what revenge he would exact.

He studied her briefly, then suddenly capitulated. 'It is a shade warm in here. I'll roll down a window.'

# CHAPTER SEVEN

AS SOON as Gary turned away, Charlotte pulled up the handle and gave the door a hearty shove. Literally throwing herself out of the car, she stumbled, caught her balance, then started to run. The moon had dipped behind a cloud and it was like speeding into a black void. Behind her, though, she could hear Gary swearing, and she didn't slow down—until she ran into a bale of hay. She fell headlong over the obstruction, landing face down on the far side of it. Winded, she lay breathlessly waiting for the sound of approaching footsteps. The stubble of the new-cut alfalfa was like lying on a bed of nails; it dug into her skin in a million pinpricks. But she didn't dare move. Gary was out of the car now; she could hear him stumbling around, calling after her.

She felt as though she'd been lying there holding her breath for hours when finally he yelled out, 'All right, you stupid bitch! You can just stay out here all night if that's the way you want it.' The car door slammed and he reversed the vehicle down the lane in a spray of sand. She heard him rev the motor as he gained the road, then the dying roar of the engine as he sped away.

Stiffly, Charlotte got to her feet. In the distance, she could see the fading red of his tail-lights as Gary headed back towards the Mitchell ranch. Her hands trembling from reaction, she gingerly brushed off the twigs of hay and sand-burrs clinging to her clothes. Her arms smarted from a dozen scratches and one elbow throbbed where she'd landed on it.

As she straightened again, the moon slid out of the patch of cloud it had been hiding behind and bathed the hay field in its silver glow. She was several yards off the track, a couple of hundred feet from the road. The landscape was dotted with the dark shapes of hay bales, and mosquitoes buzzed around her face. She brushed them away, grimacing. 'Well, this is a fine mess you've gotten yourself into,' she said aloud. They'd driven several miles from the Mitchell ranch before Gary had pulled into this field, but God only knew how much further it was from here back into Boulder.

Feet dragging, she slowly walked back up to the track. Undoubtedly, the ranch would be closer, but she just couldn't face anyone there: Gary, the Mitchells—oh, lord, Harris and his fiancée were there too! It would just be too humiliating, after the look Harris had given her when Gary had kissed her at the party, to have him find out about this little escapade!

Before she reached the road, Charlotte detoured off the track and sat down on a bale to think over her situation. For one dreadful moment her thoughts veered to those minutes in the car with Gary, the obvious outcome of that encounter had she not got away. Bile rose in her throat, and helplessly she fell to her knees and retched. Waves of nausea washed over her as a cold sweat broke out on her forehead. When finally the sickness passed, she felt spent, her eyes awash with tears.

She turned to lean against the bale, blinking furiously to clear her vision. 'Don't think about it,' she commanded herself. 'Worry about getting home, that's the main thing.' A sob rose up in her throat and she choked it back.

Looking over to the road, she asked herself jokingly, 'So when do you think the next bus will be along?' It didn't cheer her up much. Out here, she had a better chance of catching a lift with a UFO than with a bus. Public transport didn't service the back of beyond.

Not that she could pay the fare anyway, she realised. Her bag was still in Gary's car as far as she knew. She couldn't even comb her hair, she thought fretfully, her control threatened as she pulled her fingers through the tangled mess.

Realising that she was on the verge of dissolving into tears, she made herself get up and start towards the road. She had a long walk in front of her, and self-pity wasn't going to shorten it.

She'd almost reached the public thoroughfare when the sound of an approaching car shattered the night stillness. For a second she considered running out to flag it down, then immediately rejected the idea. After what had happened tonight with Gary, she couldn't possibly risk accepting a lift from a stranger.

Standing where she was, she waited for the car to pass. It was going at speed, but seemed to slow down as it neared the entrance to the field. It wasn't until the headlights swept towards her in a broad arc though that she realised it was turning in. For an instant she was held transfixed in the harsh beam of light, then she spun on her heel and ran. Only one person knew she was here, and she wasn't waiting around to find out what he'd come back for.

The car door slammed behind her, and someone called out her name. Panicking, she strove to go faster, dodging bales and ruts as she ran. Her lungs were bursting, yet she could hear the footfalls gaining on her. She was half crazed with fear when suddenly there was a crash behind her, then an angry male voice swearing violently.

It was that voice that checked her headlong rush. Drawing to a halt, she cautiously turned around and looked towards the dark shape of a man sprawled on the ground several feet behind her. 'Harris?'

She was answered by a series of groans and curses, but they made her more certain of the identity of her pursuer. Taking a step forward, she called again, 'Harris, is that you?'

'Of course it's me,' he snapped. 'Who else would be stupid enough to go charging through a pitch-black hay field in the dead of night after a scatterbrained idiot?' He hauled himself to his feet, exclaiming, 'Ouch!' when he stood upright. Hobbling, he staggered over to a bale and sank down on to it. When Charlotte reached him, he was peering down at his foot, slowly rotating it at the ankle.

'Are you all right?'

'I only wrenched it. It should be OK in a minute.' His tone was curt and impatient and did nothing to set her at ease. An awkward silence ensued, during which Harris removed his shoe and massaged his ankle.

Feeling superfluous, Charlotte watched him. She would have liked to help, but his attitude was far from welcoming.

She was just getting around to wondering how he had found her out here when Harris slipped his shoe back on and looked up at her. 'How about you? Are you all right?'

Just the way he said it, his silvery eyes searching her face, convinced her that he must have some idea of what had gone on with Gary. It had been a frightening, degrading experience, the kind of thing she never wanted anyone to find out about, least of all Harris. Feeling sick with humiliation, she muttered, 'I'm OK.'

His earlier irritation had vanished and he said gently, 'You don't sound too sure.' When she shrugged, he edged along the bale and patted the place next to him. 'Come sit down for a minute. I want to rest my ankle before going back to the car.'

Reluctantly, Charlotte did as she was bade, gingerly sitting down at the far edge of the bale, her arms crossed awkwardly in front of her. A slight breeze had sprung up and the scent of new-mown hay was all around them. A cricket chirped; somewhere in the distance a dog barked. She couldn't look at Harris, and it seemed he had nothing to say. Her nerves were stretching and finally she burst out, 'I suppose you're going to tell me I deserved it!'

'Did you?' he asked quietly.

'No, I didn't!' she cried, a shudder going through her. The tears she'd held at bay so far were close to the surface, threatening to break free. 'I. . .all I wanted was for him to take me home. I never thought. . .' She shook her head and a tear spilled down her cheek.

Moving closer, Harris slipped his arm around her shoulders and cradled her against his shoulder. Stroking her hair in a soothing gesture, he asked, 'What exactly happened?'

She choked back a sob, battling to regain her composure. Harris's quiet strength helped bolster her and eventually she was able to answer. 'Nothing really, I guess. I don't know why I'm making such a fuss. . .he just pulled in here, stopped the car. I mean. . .' She laughed, but there was an edge of hysteria to it. 'I thought he had to be kidding. Mature adults just don't park in any old convenient spot and start making out in the car!' she gulped, looking up into Harris's face. His eyes were shadowed in the dim light, but their warmth and reassurance came through.

'Go on,' he prompted gently.

'Well, he parked. . .he even put the seat down. I told him to take me home and he got kind of nasty. I let him kiss me. . .and then. . .I told him I was hot and when he moved to open the window I ran away.'

'So nothing. . .he didn't. . .'

Charlotte shook her head and a tremor ran through her. It had been such a close call. Harris's arm tightened about her offering comfort. She tipped her head back to look up at him. In the moonlight, his face was chiselled planes of dark and light, his thoughts and expression hidden. How could she confess that she hadn't wanted to go out with Gary in the first place? That she'd only agreed because he, Harris, had been there, that in her secret heart she'd hoped to make him jealous?

His silence was oppression, and finally she cried miserably, 'What happened was all my own fault really. I. . .I should have accepted your offer to drive me home,' she admitted.

He lifted his hand and ran his fingertips down the curve of her cheek, wiping away the dampness of tears. 'It wasn't your fault, Charlotte. You showed poor judgement in your choice of escorts, but that doesn't excuse his behaviour. No man has the right to force a woman, whatever the circumstances. He ought to be. . .' His jaw firmed into a tight, angry line, and his hand fell away, clenching into a hard fist.

Ultra-sensitive in the aftermath of her ordeal, Charlotte reacted to his wrath, quailing from him. Immediately he was remorseful, gathering her to him and calming her fretful nerves. As her trembling ceased, he slipped his hand beneath her chin and lifted her face to his. 'Feeling better now?'

Her lashes were wet and spiky, but her tears were drying and she managed a tentative smile. 'Yes,' she whispered. His mouth touched hers in a soft kiss, then he let his hand fall to her shoulder.

Charlotte stared up into his eyes, willing him to go on kissing her. His touch was a cleansing lotion, his embrace a healing balm. She needed him, his comfort. . .his love. . .to blot out the degradation and ugliness of her experience.

He held her gaze, his eyes unreadable. They were cast in shadow, with only the occasional glint of moonlight reflecting from their depths. 'Oh, Charlotte, don't look at me like that.' Against his will, he lowered his head again, his mouth covering the soft sweetness of hers in a long, endearing kiss. Charlotte drowned in it, letting it wash away the unhappy memories, the feeling of humiliation.

At last he released her, holding her back from him with his hands on her shoulders. For a long moment, he searched her moonlit features, then abruptly dropped his arms to his sides. 'We'd better get going.' He stood, easing his weight on to his injured ankle, then walked towards his car with a slight limp.

She watched him go, feeling suddenly lost and abandoned. It had been a special moment, a special kiss, but it was over now and not to be repeated. After all, Harris was engaged to someone else. Scrambling to her feet, Charlotte hurried after him, catching him up when he'd almost reached the car. 'I forgot to ask you: where's Janice?' The appalling thought that his fiancée might have been waiting in the car for them all this time had just occurred to her.

Harris hesitated a fraction and Charlotte looked at him, but his face was averted. Finally, he said, 'We. . .she decided to stay over at the Mitchells'.' At his companion's enquiring silence, he added shortly, 'They're old family friends.'

'I see,' Charlotte murmured, not seeing at all. From Janice's reponse when Harris had offered to drive her home from the party before, she'd had the impression that they would also be leaving it together at the end of the evening. Something had changed their plans.

Harris was by the door and had it open for her, waiting for her to get in. She quickened her pace and slid into the seat. As she fumbled for the seatbelt, she glanced up to see Harris's face illuminated by the interior light just before he slammed the door shut.

Distracted, she finished fastening the belt, watching his dark figure move around the car to the driver's side. As soon as he had settled behind the wheel, she exclaimed, 'Did you do that when you tripped in the field?' She pointed to his face. With only moonlight to see by, she hadn't noticed the bruising around one of his eyes, but in the brighter light from the car it was obvious that Harris was sporting one hell of a shiner!

His movements deliberate, he reached forward and turned on the engine. Craning his neck to see while he backed down the lane to the road, he said brusquely, 'It happened earlier.'

His tone didn't invite further speculation, and Charlotte watched him curiously. As they gained the road and he put the car in drive to go on, she noticed by the light from the dashboard that the knuckles on his hands were bruised as well. She couldn't contain herself. 'You were in a fight!' she announced.

Annoyance was etched in every line of his profile as he concentrated on the road. When it became obvious that he didn't intend to tender any explanation, she found herself asking, 'Who. . .what happened?'

He sent her a harassed look, then sighed impatiently. 'Well, how do you think I got Gary to tell me where he'd dumped you?'

'You mean. . .you had a fight with *Gary*?' she squeaked in astonishment.

'Doesn't that give you an ego thrill?' he charged sardonically.

'Of course not, but——' She stopped abruptly, her thoughts churning.

'And in answer to your next question,' he anticipated her churlishly, 'no, Janice was *not* thrilled. We had a big row afterwards and she decided to spend a few days with the Mitchells!' Charlotte wasn't given much opportunity to digest that bit of information when he indicted bitterly, 'I knew the minute I saw you again that you were going to be trouble!'

'Me?' she exclaimed. 'But I wasn't even there!'

'But you were the root cause of the whole mess—all because you had to go out with that jerk—insisted on his driving you home. I embarrassed the Mitchells, my fiancée—just to get you out of the scrap you were in!'

'You said before that it wasn't my fault that Gary. . .'

He was silent for a moment, before finally relenting. 'I know I said that, and I did mean it,' he said heavily. 'None the less, you were damn lucky. When I left the party, I didn't know what I was going to find. It was a very hard few minutes before I got to you. Gary was pretty drunk and wasn't too clear on exactly what had happened. I was afraid he might have beaten you up—left you lying half dead out in that field.' He paused as he turned on to the highway, then continued derisively, 'Instead, you took off on me like a scared jack-rabbit!'

'I'm sorry,' she offered meekly, and he shot her a sardonic glance that quelled further apologies. As she didn't really know what else she could say to him, she maintained an uncomfortable silence as they sped towards the city. She felt incredibly guilty. She'd had a nasty few moments with Gary, but all in all she'd come out of them relatively unscathed. Poor Harris, though, she thought, sending him a loving look. A black eye, bruised knuckles, a wrenched ankle—she frowned slightly. Probably what bothered him more than any physical discomfort was his quarrel with his fiancée.

As they entered the outskirts of Boulder, Harris asked for directions to her apartment. She told him the street to take, then a couple of minutes later realised that, as he'd driven her home before, he should know where she lived. It was rather dampening to think that he was so indifferent to her that he didn't remember.

While 'thrilled' was too strong a word to describe her reaction to learning he'd fought Gary over her, she had not been unmoved. She wouldn't have been human had she not been somewhat gratified by the way he'd rushed to her rescue. Apparently there had been nothing personal in his knight errancy, though. He'd admitted he had thought Gary had harmed her. His action had probably been nothing more than common chivalry—he would have done the same for any woman he'd thought was in trouble.

Feeling slightly quashed, Charlotte pointed out the street where they should next turn. Harris veered on to it, then asked, 'You're still living in the same place?'

'Yes, of course.' She slid him a puzzled look. When he didn't elaborate, she said, 'I haven't moved. Why would you think I had?'

'I just thought you might have.' He kept his eyes on the road and when they reached the next turning, steered the car round it. They were only a block from her apartment when he said, 'So I guess your boyfriend moved out, then.'

It took her a minute to figure out who he meant, then she asked, 'You mean Jimmy?'

'If that's the name of the guy you were living with.'

'Jimmy hasn't gone anywhere.'

'I see,' he said grimly, sliding the car into a vacant parking slot. Putting it out of gear, he turned his head to study her, the contempt in his expression apparent even in the darkened car. 'You really are something, you know that?'

Cautiously, Charlotte eyed him. 'What do you mean?'

'I mean, Jimmy—who you live with; Gary—who you went out to have *fun* with—I'm beginning to wonder just what really happened when he was taking you home. Then I guess I had better add myself to the list. You haven't exactly been an ice maiden when I've been around. Out there in that hay field tonight, I thought for a minute that you might go up in flames.'

She hated him for saying that. It had been a special moment for her—and now he'd ruined it. He caught her eyes in a steady gaze of derision, his mouth curled with contempt. Suddenly, she was more angry than she could ever remember being.

*She* wasn't engaged, she wasn't planning to marry anyone. 'You're nothing but a hypocritical rake. Jimmy and I understand one another. *I'm* not cheating on him. He doesn't care how many men I go out with, how many I *kiss*!' She glared at him with revulsion. 'Can you say the same for Janice—your *fiancée*?'

She didn't like Janice much. She found her cold and calculatingly childish, with a holier-than-thou manner about her that irritated her no end. However, she could find it in her heart to feel pity for the girl. What could be worse than marrying a man who couldn't be trusted—a wolf who chased anything in a skirt?

She didn't wait for his answer. Throwing him a final scathing look, she reached for the lever and shoved open the door. Scrambling out on to the pavement, she slammed the door and started towards the entrance to her apartment building.

As she stalked up to the building to ring the bell for Jimmy to let her in—she'd left her key in her bag, so it was still in Gary's car—she heard the car motor start. The sound of the engine had long died away by the time the old man shuffled to the door.

# CHAPTER EIGHT

CHARLOTTE rushed into the lounge the next day, only to come to an abrupt halt when she saw Harris standing at the bar with Tony. Before she could carry through her impulse to turn around and go back out of the door, Tony caught sight of her. 'Here she is now.' Harris turned to look at her, so she reluctantly finished the journey to the bar.

'Where have you been?' the bartender demanded as soon as she reached them. 'You're over an hour late.'

Charlotte sneaked a quick glance at Harris, wincing inwardly when she saw his black eye. The Black Stallion had been better when the lighting was bad. Unwilling to continue looking at him, she gave her explanation to the bartender. 'My car wouldn't start, so I had to take the bus, and I missed a connection.'

As Tony made sympathetic noises, she tried to stifle her guilt. Her car hadn't started simply because the key was in her bag and she'd forgotten it was still with Gary until it was time to leave for work.

'Mr Jordan and I were just going to call someone in to take your shift,' Tony explained, handing her a tray and her float. As she reached out to take it, he looked curiously at her arm, then at Harris. Grinning suddenly, he teased, 'You two must have been at the same party last night.'

Stunned by his perception, Charlotte's hands froze

on the tray. Surely, Harris wouldn't think she'd blabbed to Tony about that fiasco last night! She slid him a fearful glance as he asked frigidly, 'And what makes you say that?'

Quelled by his employer's coldness, Tony shifted uncomfortably and said, 'Well—er—just look at you both.' Not daring to point to his boss's injuries, he drew attention to Charlotte's. There were a couple of ugly scratches running down her forearm where the hay stubble had caught her, but it was the livid black and blue mark just below the cuff of her short-sleeved blouse that really stood out.

An uneasy silence ensued as Charlotte became aware of Harris's frowning inspection of the bruise. Squirming beneath his regard, she pulled the tray from the counter, saying, 'Well, I'd better get to work.'

Aware of the tension, if not its cause, Tony echoed the thought. 'Me, too,' he announced, and bustled off to the other end of the bar to wash some glasses.

Charlotte would have left too, only Harris's restraining hand prevented her. Gently tracing the bruise with his fingertips, he asked huskily, 'Did Sanders do that?'

His caress was a firebrand, melting her bones and turning her blood to liquid heat. Trying to ignore the traitorous sensations his touch aroused, she looked up into his eyes. 'Yes,' she whispered.

His jaw tightened, a look of savage anger arrowing briefly through his silvery eyes. 'Well, then, I don't regret what I did to him,' he admitted grimly. His hand lingered over her injury, soothing it with his touch and drawing her into his web of attraction. The spell was broken though as he pulled his hand away and eyed her with sternly set features.

'I hope you learned your lesson,' he said harshly. 'I might not always be around to bail you out, so next time one of your customers asks you out, maybe you'll have the good sense to turn him down.'

Stung by his sudden condemnation, she reacted with impertinence. 'Is that an order, Mr Jordan?'

'It could be.'

'Well, then, I'll make a note of it,' she retorted acidly, swinging around on her heel and stalking out into the lounge.


'This is getting ludicrous. People are going to think we're running a first-aid station here.' At the bartender's comment, Charlotte looked up from her order pad, then back behind her to see what had captured his attention.

What she saw was Gary slowly making his way to a table—at least that was who she thought it was, but his face was so battered she couldn't be positive. One side of his jaw was swollen out like an aubergine, the skin mottled in shades of violet and blue. A strip of plaster covered the bridge of his nose and his right eye was blackened and swollen completely shut.

When she turned back to the bar, she found Tony watching her intently. 'Isn't that the guy you were talking to in here the other night?' he asked.

God, Tony had a memory like an elephant's! Hedging, Charlotte shrugged, saying, 'Maybe.'

'It's some coincidence, isn't it?' the bartender ruminated. 'Him looking like that. . .your arm all banged up and Mr Jordan looking as if a truck ran over him?'

It wasn't phrased as a question, but Tony was probing none the less. Charlotte tossed him a disgruntled look and said quickly, 'Well, I'd better go get his order.'

As she moved reluctantly towards Gary's table, she wished there had been some way she could have avoided ever seeing him again. However, she needed her bag back.

When she reached his table and had a better look at his face though, she found her hostility dying. It must have been some fight. The poor man—he looked as if a pit bull terrier had savaged him. Normally, Gary was a very good-looking fellow, and well aware of it. His ego must be pretty battered as well at having to go around looking like this. It was shocking to think that Harris had beaten another human being to such an extent.

'Hello, Gary. What can I get you?'

He wouldn't meet her eyes. 'Hi,' he muttered, his swollen lips barely moving. 'I don't want anything to drink. I just came in to give you your bag.' He reached down beside his chair and brought up the handbag.

She took it from him, feeling awkward with pity. After what he'd tried to do to her, it was ridiculous to feel sorry for him, but she couldn't help herself. 'Sure you wouldn't like a beer or something?'

'Can't drink anything without a straw,' he mumbled. 'I'd feel silly slurping down a beer with one.'

'Well, OK, then.' She bit her lip, watching him. Finally, she said, 'I guess I'll get back to work. Thanks for bring my bag to me.'

'Least I could do.' He cleared his throat uncertainly.

'I. . .er. . .guess I owe you an apology for last night. I wasn't going to hurt you, I wouldn't have. . . Well, you know how chicks are. . .they say no but they don't really mean it.'

He wouldn't win any prizes for contrition, Charlotte decided, feeling her animosity returning. He probably deserved the trouncing Harris had given him! 'I *did* mean it,' she said coldly. Having nothing further to say to him, she stalked off towards the bar.

She'd nearly reached it when out of the corner of her eye she saw the lounge door coming from the lobby open. Reprieve! With another customer to wait on, she could delay having to deal with Tony and his infernal curiosity!

Charlotte swung around to assess the newcomer, stopping dead in her tracks when she saw who it was. Janice, all smiles, was heading straight for Gary's table. When she got there, Charlotte heard her say, 'I've gotten everything packed. The bellboy's taking it down to the car right now. Are you ready to go?'

The girl stretched out a solicitous hand and slipped it under Gary's elbow to help him to his feet. Shepherding him along like a bantam hen with one lone chick, she manoeuvred him towards the exit. 'You really shouldn't have insisted on coming into town with me,' she scolded him prettily. 'When we get home you're going straight back to bed!'

Her lips parted slightly in astonishment, Charlotte watched the exit door swing shut behind the couple. After a moment she turned back to the bar. Tony was staring at the exit door, looking as dumbfounded as she felt. When she walked up, though, he turned his attention to her. 'If you don't tell me what's going on, I'll. . .' He shook his head, casting another disbelieving look towards the exit.

Charlotte moistened her lips, then said, 'I don't know anything about that.' Obviously, he didn't believe her, even if she was telling the truth. Before he could tackle her, she set her tray on the counter and picked up a handful of change. 'I think I'll go put some money in the juke-box. It's awfully quiet in here tonight.'

It stayed quiet, even with the juke-box going, and was one of those interminable evenings that dragged on leaden feet. They never had more than a half a dozen customers at any one time, and there were several periods when there wasn't anyone at all.

During college times, Charlotte would have used the slow evening to catch up on her homework. But she was on vacation, so she ended up feeding money into the juke-box most of the evening. She couldn't really afford it, but Tony was annoyed with her for her caginess and it allowed her to avoid the bar.

Later on, she had a more pressing reason for wanting to stay out in the lounge area. Around nine o'clock, Harris came back into the Black Stallion and sat down on a stool at the end of the bar. He ordered a beer and spent the rest of the night staring into it. His obvious dejection, not to mention his battered face, tore at her heart. On the other hand, she couldn't bring herself to offer sympathy when he was only down because his fiancée had walked out on him. That would be asking a little too much.

So she stuck another quarter in the juke-box, then

went to the bar to fetch a refill for their only other customer. As she waited for Tony to mix the drink, her gaze was drawn compulsively to Harris. His arms were resting on the counter, dark and strong below the rolled sleeves of his pale blue sports shirt. His hands were long-fingered, the nails neatly trimmed. They were big hands, powerful, and yet she knew they could be infinitely gentle.

Charlotte started guiltily when suddenly Harris spoke. It was only to snarl, 'Do you have to keep playing that lousy music?'

She threw him a dirty look and turned her back to him. The words of the song filtered into her consciousness and she felt a twinge of guilt. She hadn't even realised she'd punched up one of the few remaining country and western records on the box. Come to think of it, the woeful ballad of lost love didn't exactly improve her mood either!

When Tony brought her the drink, he said, 'Look, why don't you deliver this then go on home? It's a waste of time for us both to be here when it's so slow.'

Charlotte hesitated, then glanced at her watch. Tony must have forgotten she didn't have her car. She supposed she could make the next bus, though, if she hurried. 'OK, sure. I'll drop this off, then go,' she agreed finally.

As she picked up her tray, he said, 'Oh, I forgot. You don't have your car.'

'I'll take the bus.'

He frowned. 'Are you sure? It's after eleven—it's kind of late for you to be taking public transport,

Charlie. It might be better for you to just stay on and I'll give you a lift home after we close.'

Charlotte paused, considering. Now that the opportunity of escape had presented itself, she couldn't wait to leave. With Harris hovering at the end of the bar like the skeleton at the feast, it was hardly a congenial atmosphere.

On the other hand, she didn't like taking the bus late at night. The whole idea made her nervous.

Before she could come to a decision, Harris stood up and walked over to them. 'I'll drive Charlotte home,' he announced.

'You don't——'

'That'll solve the problem,' Tony cut her off, looking relieved.

Dismayed, Charlotte gave her friend a disgruntled look and an even more furious one to Harris. They might have at least consulted her!

'I would rather——'

This time it was Harris who interrupted. 'Hadn't you better serve that drink before the ice melts?' he asked in a very boss-like tone. Her lips set, she glared at him and he smiled slightly. 'That's a good girl. Maybe I'll buy you a cup of coffee before I take you home. I'll wait for you in the employees' lounge while you finish up here.'

He'd gone before she could untangle her tongue enough to recommend he go somewhere a lot hotter. Frustrated, she snatched up the drink and stalked over to the man waiting for it.

She was still fuming when she entered the employees' lounge a few minutes later. Harris was seated at a table, idly flipping through an out-of-date magazine. He set it aside as she came in, giving her an enquiring look.

She told him, her voice shaking with anger. 'I'll take a cab. I don't want you to take me home.' Not waiting for his answer, she stormed over to her locker and took out her street clothes.

When she turned back, she found Harris scrutinising her with mild interest. 'Why not?' he asked.

'Because. . .' She had to stop there. She didn't really know why. . .or at least she did, but she couldn't tell him. He'd been moping over Janice all night and he only wanted to console himself with her now. As his dark brow lifted in ironic enquiry, an idea struck and she said sweetly, 'Because I don't date the patrons of the bar any more. Boss's orders!'

He gave her a sardonic look, conceding, 'I suppose I deserved that.'

His admission took the wind right out of her sails. As she stood regarding him uncertainly, he said, 'I really want to take you, though, and. . .' he smiled crookedly '. . .the boss'll give you permission to go if you think you need it.'

Her expression was unyielding, although inside she warred with the desire to prolong their encounter. The trouble was, Harris was just too damn charming when he wanted to be, plucking a responsive chord within her that she wished would stay silent.

He was even more compelling when he lowered his head and ran his hand over the nape of his neck in a distracted manner that extracted compassion from her heart. When he looked up at her again, the bruise around his eye seemed even darker against his face, his eyes old and sad. Lines of weariness etched his countenance, reflecting every one of his twenty-nine years and then some. She knew she was losing the battle to reject him.

'Is it so much to ask, Charlotte? Couldn't we just go out, have a cup of coffee together without getting into an argument, then I'll drive you home? No funny stuff, either. I promise.'

Helplessly, she gazed into the ghostly stillness of his grey eyes, knowing she was too weak to resist his appeal. She was in love with him, dammit. He was only feeling sad and down in the mouth because of Janice, but. . . So what if he was only using her as a substitute—someone to keep him company through this bad patch? Even knowing she was looking to get hurt all over again, she nodded in agreement.

One could have said it was the start of a beautiful friendship, but that would have been an exaggeration. Certainly, in the nights that followed, they shared many a cup of coffee in the late-night diner down the street from the Foothills. However, there was a restraint to their relationship, a wariness that kept both of them from feeling totally at ease.

They talked about their lives—their lives now, never the past—Harris about his work, his aspirations; Charlotte about her schooling and hopes for her teaching career. By unspoken pact, though, there were subjects that were never broached. Janice was one. She hadn't come back to the Foothills, but various people had seen her around town, usually in the company of

Gary. The grapevine hummed with her doings, but there was no way Charlotte felt she could ask Harris what the situation was—and he never mentioned his fiancée, or was it *ex*-fiancée now?

Jimmy was another subject that was avoided. Actually, she would have liked to discuss the old man with Harris. He was starting to become a continual source of worry to Charlotte as his mental faculties deteriorated. She knew in her heart that a crisis was looming, but was loath to accept it. She would have liked to talk it over with someone. However, whenever she tried to steer the subject in that direction with Harris, to clear up his misunderstanding of her relationship with Jimmy, he deftly tacked away from it.

Oddly enough, her job at the Black Stallion was another subject Harris sidestepped. He owned the hotel, should have been interested in what went on in the lounge and how his innovations were working out, but for some reason he didn't want her talking about it. Whenever she tried, he very pointedly changed the subject.

Despite the restrictions, at least they were talking. That was something they'd seldom done in the past. During those heady weeks of their earlier affair, they'd been too wrapped up in the physical delights of their relationship for conversation. Since meeting again, it seemed they'd spent most of their time fighting instead of communicating. As the days passed, Charlotte found herself drawing closer and closer to Harris, her love deepening.

The platonic nature of this new arrangement did give her cause for some heartache, however. For her, the

physical attraction, the awareness of him, was still as
strong as ever. She ever began to wonder if he'd lost
interest in her, in that way. However, an incident a few
nights later told her differently.

He was escorting her back to the hotel car park to
pick up her car when she stumbled on a rough patch of
pavement. She would have gone headlong to the
ground, but his firm arm, catching her by the waist,
saved her from the accident.

Shaken, Charlotte took a moment to still the frantic
pulsing of her heart in the aftermath of the near
accident, leaning against his firm chest and barely
aware that his arm was still around her. When she'd
calmed down, she looked up into his face and her heart
lurched, again beating at double time. His eyes held an
intensity, a painful awareness that couldn't be denied.
She could see in them that he wanted her as much as
she desired him.

Moistening her lips, she tipped her head up, whisper-
ing, 'Harris?' There was a hard ache in the pit of her
stomach as she willed him to cover her lips with his
own, to assuage the deep need she had for his touch.

For a long, breathless minute he peered down into
her pleading eyes, struggling against their spell. She
knew he was weakening, when suddenly a car passed
by the adjoining street, the hiss of its tyres rolling along
the asphalt, shattering the moment. Abruptly he
released her, side-stepping to put a couple of feet
between them.

'It's getting pretty late. I'd better be getting you back
to your car.'

Feeling hurt and bewildered, Charlotte stayed where

she was as he walked on. When he looked back over his shoulder, one dark brow cocked in enquiry, she pulled herself together and hurried to catch up.

At her car, Harris took the keys from her and held the door open for her to slide in behind the wheel. She hesitated a moment, looking up at him, unaware that her feelings were reflected in her expression. Her mouth drooped in a desolate pout; her violet eyes shadowed bruises set in a sad, pale face.

'Well, goodnight,' she said huskily, reluctant to leave him.

'Goodnight,' he echoed, giving her no choice but to get into the car. She'd half turned from him when he touched her arm, and she swung back round. 'Goodnight, Charlotte,' he repeated, sliding his arms around her and enfolding her in them. For several moments he simply held her, drawn against his chest, their hearts beating as one. Her head was cradled in the hollow of his shoulder, his warmth, his closeness encasing her in a blanket of security.

Finally, though, he released her, looking down into her eyes, his own softly grey and touched with sadness. 'We're going to have to do something about us,' he whispered enigmatically. Slowly, his head dropped, his lips touching hers in a gentle kiss, tender and infinitely sweet.

She savoured his touch, her hands against his broad shoulders, her body blending into his. She wanted to submerge herself in him, prolong the caress for an eternity, but all too soon he was putting her away from him.

For a brief moment his eyes touched hers, then he

dropped his gaze. 'Goodnight,' he said once again, something remote in his tone. 'Take care on the drive home.'

Abruptly, he turned his back to her and, skirting the car, walked towards the back entrance of the hotel. Following his progress, Charlotte swivelled her head to keep him in view. The sulphur lights of the car park painted a golden aura around him, setting his dark head alight, and shining across his broad shoulders.

When he reached the entrance to the building, he turned back. Unaccountably embarrassed, Charlotte gave him a quick salute, then slid quickly into her car and fired the motor. At that distance, he couldn't possibly have read the love and longing in her expression.

She only drove a block from the hotel before pulling over and resting her head against the wheel. What had he meant about doing something about themselves? Did it mean he was going to finish with Janice, remove that barrier standing between them? Or did he mean he was going to finish with *her*?

# CHAPTER NINE

WHEN Charlotte went on shift the next day, she hesitated a moment at the entry door, surveying the lounge. It was fairly crowded for the time of day, but then she'd noticed a steady increase in business lately—ever since Harris had taken over the management of the hotel, in fact. He was a good businessman, she thought with pride. Not content with merely giving the hotel a face-lift, he had ensured that no minor details would be overlooked that might destroy the ambience of the Foothills. Since his hiring of a different cleaning firm, the whole complex seemed to sparkle with a new brightness. Fresh flowers graced the public rooms at all times and landscapes by local artists had turned the lobby into a mini-gallery. Poor Annabelle, the Black Stallion's nude, had been relegated to a store-room while a more tasteful and appropriate painting was sought.

Other changes more directly affecting the staff had been enacted as well. The new, more practical uniforms for the bar staff had only been a start. Whereas under the previous management you couldn't take a day off sick without losing by it, when Tony's wife, Ann, had had a baby last week, Harris had called Tony in and given him three weeks' paternity leave with pay in order to let him settle down with the new addition.

Some of the older members of the staff were shocked

by Harris's liberal policies—this new owner was too
soft, would run the Foothills into bankruptcy. However, the younger staff appreciated his enlightened
attitude and morale had never been higher. The
Foothills was gaining the reputation as a great place to
work, and those who had jobs there did them with
pride and enthusiasm.

Unfortunately, the atmosphere of friendliness and
camaraderie had done nothing to mitigate the rumour-
mill. When Charlotte reached the bar, Linda rushed
up, positively bursting with the latest juicy titbit to
regale Charlotte with.

'You've just got to hear about Mr Jordan!' the
younger girl exclaimed.

Charlotte slid her a cautious look, making a show of
getting her tray ready so she could go out on to the
floor. Harris was probably the best boss the Foothills
had ever had. It was annoying the way his ungrateful
employees still insisted on prying into every detail of
his life. If someone had seen him kissing her in the car
park last night and Linda started going on about it,
she'd probably murder the girl.

'I wish I'd been in the dining-room at noon. Rachel
only heard a fraction of the conversation but. . .'

Thank God no one had seen them last night! The
only one at the hotel who knew she and Harris had
been meeting each other after work was Tony. He
could be relied on to keep it to himself, but the rest of
this crew! It would be humiliating to know your every
move was being dissected by a bunch of tongue-
wagging scandalmongers!

Although obviously she wasn't featured in today's

headlines, Charlotte snapped at Linda anyway. 'Don't you think it's rather rude and pathetic to eavesdrop on someone's private conversation, then go spreading what you hear all around the hotel?'

Linda's face had crumbled to one of sulky martyrdom. 'It wasn't all that private,' she pouted. 'Rachel said they were practically shouting at one another.'

'That still doesn't mean she should have been hanging on to every word,' Charlotte charged.

Before she could remind the girl to mind her own business and let Harris mind his, Linda whined, 'But we've all been wondering what was going on with him and his fiancée.'

The homily died in Charlotte's throat. Harris loomed too large in her life, in her heart, for her to be indifferent to his activities. She'd been naturally curious on learning he'd had a disagreement with someone, but, that curiosity was flavoured with a definite distaste for idle gossip, and easily contained.

However, knowing it was Janice with whom he'd quarrelled cast a whole new light on the incident. The girl's status in his life was of vital importance to Charlotte, a burning question that had plagued her for weeks.

'He was quarrelling with Janice?' she asked the other girl offhandedly, trying to conceal her interest by casually fingering the change lying on her tray. Inside she was sick with self-disgust at her prying, but she had to know.

Linda gave her a superior look, seeing straight through her nonchalance. 'Don't tell me *you're* interested, Miss Goody Two Shoes.'

Charlotte's mouth set in a tight-lipped line. 'Maybe I am,' she admitted tautly.

'I've been wondering about you and him.' The waitress gave the older girl a sly, speculative look. 'After that night the boss drove you to the hospital to get your hand stitched, I heard you went to see him in his penthouse a couple of days later.'

She should have known the news of that visit would eventually have made the rounds. However, she wasn't going to satisfy Linda's need for details by trading them for today's bulletin. 'Just tell me what happened this afternoon,' she ordered coldly.

Linda didn't answer immediately, but savoured Charlotte's interest, taunting her with it. However, when Charlotte gave her a look of suppressed violence, she relented. 'Mr Jordan and his fiancée had lunch together. Rachel didn't hear much of what they said at first, but she thought they might be talking about that Gary fellow Janice had been seeing. Anyway, later on, they really started to argue. It seems that Janice wanted to break off the engagement, but Mr Jordan wouldn't let her. Apparently, she even took off her ring and tried to give it back to him, but he wouldn't take it. Rachel said he reached over and picked it up and shoved it back on her finger.' Linda paused for breath, and when Charlotte didn't say anything she went on, relishing the telling of her tale. 'The girl must be crazy! That cowboy she's been hanging around with could never afford a fancy ring like the emerald Mr Jordan gave her. Can you imagine her trying to hand it back to him? I think she ought to clean up her act before he dumps her—although after this afternoon it looks as if she could commit murder and he'd still take her back!'

She glanced over at Charlotte, and on seeing her face said, alarmed, 'Are you all right?'

Charlotte had to swallow a hard lump in her throat before she could answer. 'Yes. . .of course I am.'

Linda's eyes were narrowed, her broad forehead pleated in a frown as she said doubtfully, 'You look awfully pale. You're not feeling sick, are you?'

She was, actually, sick with unhappiness and disillusionment. In her secret heart, where hopes and dreams dwelt, she'd felt sure Harris had broken with Janice when she'd heard they'd argued. If he was beginning to feel something for her, surely he wouldn't want to stay engaged to another woman? It wasn't like that at all, though. Instead, *Janice* was the one who had wanted out of the engagement—and *he* wasn't letting her go.

Battling to maintain some semblance of composure, Charlotte told the other girl, 'I'm fine. . .just fine. It must be the lighting in here.' She picked up her tray, and walked out into the lounge. Her legs felt shaky and her smile was a travesty as she stopped by a table to take an order.

The routine task steadied her, though, and she felt more normal when she moved off. However, glancing up, she caught Linda watching her, her eyes boring into her. Charlotte swallowed hard. Why hadn't she had the good sense to say she wasn't feeling well? Now the girl was putting two and two together, speculating, wondering if it had been something she'd said. . .

Reluctantly, Charlotte went back to the bar. Before

Linda could start questioning her, probing, she asked the bartender, 'Can I have one of those packets of breath mints?' She stroked her fingers down her throat, glancing at Linda. 'I think you're right. I must be coming down with a summer cold—my throat's a little sore,' she lied. 'Maybe some mints will help.'

When the bartender handed her the packet, she tore it open and popped one in her mouth. She wasn't fond of peppermint, but it was small price to pay to stop Linda's conjectures. Unfortunately, as the sharp taste numbed her tongue and she left the bar again, the younger girl was still eyeing her consideringly.

Luckily, Linda had gone home for the night when Harris came into the Black Stallion later on. In fact, it was quite late. The bartender, Kevin, had already called 'last call' and only a few stragglers were left, finishing up their final drink of the night. Charlotte was clearing the dirty glasses off a table when Harris strolled in and seated himself on a stool at the end of the bar.

She saw Kevin go over to ask if he wanted a drink, but the other man shook his head and turned to catch her eye. Her tray was loaded with used glasses and overflowing ashtrays, so she was forced to go back up to the bar. She hadn't wanted to see Harris tonight—was annoyed with him for even coming in here. Other than that first evening they'd had coffee together, he hadn't met her in the Black Stallion. Instead, he waited for her in the employees' lounge until she was finished. At that time of night, there weren't many other employees around, so no one but Tony had seen them together.

Of course, if this was going to be the last night he took her out, he wouldn't care about gossip—it would die a natural death with nothing further to fuel it.

As soon as she set her tray on the counter, Harris slid off the stool and walked over to her. Out of the corner of her eye she watched his approach, not wanting to acknowledge him, but compelled by love to savour his mere presence. He was so vitally attractive, vibrant with life. He walked with easy grace, his handsome head erect and held at an unconsciously proud angle. Dressed casually in a dark blue sports shirt and tight jeans, he looked rugged, masculine and heart-stoppingly sexy.

'It looks as if you're about done here. Why don't you let Kevin finish off and we'll leave?'

Charlotte bit her lower lip, focusing on her hands resting on the counter. She clasped them together, linking the fingers in a tight web. She wanted to reach out with them and pull him to her, run her fingertips over his hard-muscled body, exploring its strength.

But tonight he was going to tell her it was over. He'd been reconciled with his fiancée and there was no room in his life for her.

'I can't tonight,' she said huskily, refusing to look at him, afraid her anguish might show in her eyes.

'You can't?' he questioned. 'Why not?'

She shrugged. 'It's late—I should be getting home.'

'It's always late when we go out after your shift,' he reminded her. 'What's so different about tonight?' She could hear the bafflement in his voice.

'Nothing. . .it's just, I want to go home tonight—I like to go straight home every night, as a matter of fact.'

'And what does that mean exactly?'

She slid him a furtive look, hiding her emotions beneath her lashes. He looked puzzled. . . disappointed—but no, that couldn't be. She was only beating him to the punch, dumping him before he dumped her. Hardening her voice and her heart, she said, 'What it sounds like. I don't want to go out with you any more after work.' A surge of resentment welled within her. She hadn't liked the idea of the hotel gossips discussing her and Harris, but suddenly the discretion of their arrangement irked her. What should Harris care about the tittle-tattle that went on around here—unless he just didn't want any of it to get back to Janice? 'I don't want to go out with you at any other time either. . .not that you've ever asked me.' Despite her efforts, some of the bitterness she was feeling crept into her tones. At his steady, questioning look, she quickly grabbed an empty tray and walked out into the lounge to clear the rest of the tables. Maybe he would be gone by the time she got back.

Of course, he wasn't.

Angrily, she set the tray down on the counter beside him, the glasses rattling. Kevin was busy in the room at the back of the bar and the sole remaining customer had just left. They were alone. 'Look,' she burst out, 'can't you take a hike? We want to close up and leave.'

'To go straight home?'

'That's right.'

His silvery grey eyes searched her face and she

dropped her lashes to conceal the expression in her violet-hued eyes. 'Is that what you really want?' he asked carefully.

'Isn't that what I've been telling you?' she snapped. He was standing close to her, and she was acutely conscious of his proximity. A few short inches were all that separated them. She only had to lift her hand to touch him.

Her control stretching, she scurried around the end of the bar to the other side. Picking up the soiled glasses she'd brought over, she began loading them into the dishwasher with noisy deliberation.

Over the clatter, Harris asked, 'Are you sure you don't want to come with me. . .or is it that someone else doesn't want you to?'

Charlotte's mouth twisted sardonically. She didn't know what he was getting at, but she'd bet Janice wouldn't be too thrilled about their midnight rendezvous!

When she remained silent, he demanded harshly, 'What is it, Charlotte? Has that guy you've been living with begun to wonder why you're coming home late? Is he getting suspicious?'

She hadn't even given Jimmy a thought. He was so absent-minded now that he wasn't usually even aware of what time she got home. Half the time, she wasn't even sure he knew she'd been gone. However, Harris didn't know about her old friend's limitations, and she seized on the excuse he offered her—anything to end this confrontation.

'It's something like that,' she admitted.

He gave her an assessing look, his firm, sensual lips

set in a hard line. 'Charlotte,' he began, forcing her to meet his eyes before he continued. 'Charlotte, don't you think it's time you took stock of that relationship—thought about ending it? You can't be that happy with this Jimmy. If you were, you'd never have gone out with me in the first place. You and I. . .' He trailed off and his eyes held hers in a steady gaze, binding her with compelling intentness.

She could feel her heart hammering in her chest with suffocating force, trapping her breath in her throat as she waited for him to continue. Linda could have got that scene in the restaurant all wrong—it wouldn't be the first time the gossips had turned things around: the wealthy Arab oil sheikh who'd turned out to be a vacuum cleaner salesman from Omaha; the movie starlet who was only a housewife from Topeka. . . The misinformation that flowed through the hotel was legendary.

So she waited for him to continue, to declare himself, but in the end he only said lamely, 'It sounds like a bad scene. You should get out of it.' He looked away from her, idly tracing a pattern on the bar-counter with one finger.

Charlotte watched him, her dreams crumbling, the fragments lying at her feet. As the silence closed around them, a burning anger built within her. 'Why should I leave Jimmy? So I can go drink coffee with you after work?' she demanded sarcastically.

'That's not what I was getting at and you know it. I think the guy's bad for you.'

'Do you, now? I happen to love him.' She saw him blanch and steeled herself not to soften towards him.

She could have guessed he wanted her—that kiss last night confirmed it. But what did he want her for—a little hole-and-corner affair that wouldn't impinge on his engagement?

She said, 'My refusal to go out with you has nothing to do with him, though. Jimmy's an old man. . .he's eighty-five and a little senile. There's nothing like that going on between him and me—and there isn't going to be between us, either!'

He stared at her long and hard for a breathless minute. 'Are you saying that man, this fellow you live with, is a—a. . .?' He stumbled to a halt and she flung him a derisive look.

'He's a senior citizen,' she supplied for him. 'So what do you think of that?'

'Why, you little. . . You've enjoyed yourself, making a fool of me, haven't you?' he accused her angrily, and her mocking smile was his confirmation. It was a lie, of course. If she'd hurt him by her deception, she'd hurt herself even more. That was the way it was when you hurt someone you loved, but sometimes pride required sacrifices.

'You let me think he was your lover,' Harris continued harshly.

'I know what you thought,' she informed him. 'I didn't care. . .I don't now.'

'Charlotte.' He forced her gaze to his, locking on to it. 'We could have——'

'We could have what? Had a *ménage à trois*?' she interrupted frigidly. 'You tell *me* the truth now. . .are you still engaged to Janice?'

He hesitated, his mouth set rigidly. Finally, he answered quietly and simply, 'Yes.'

Even though she'd known the answer, she still felt the pain of a knife-wound to her heart. Rallying, she asked hoarsely, 'Is it true that she tried to break it off this afternoon and you wouldn't let her?'

'You heard about that?'

'Everybody in the whole damn hotel heard about it!' she exploded. 'So it *is* true.'

He gave her a harried look, then rested his chin in his hand and stroked his jawline with his thumb. Finally, he dropped his hand and said to her, 'I can explain, Charlotte.'

'But it *is* true!'

'Yes, OK, it's true, but it's not what you're thinking. . .'

'You wouldn't want to know my thoughts!' she advised him stormily. 'Get out of here! Leave me alone. . .I don't want to have anything more to do with you!'

Angry colour crept up his face, his eyes diamond-hard. 'I have a right to explain!'

'Oh, I can imagine. Let me guess. . .she doesn't understand you?' she suggested acidly. 'I'm not a naïve little seventeen-year-old any more. I was so stupid to think a man like you would ever care for someone like me. All you wanted was somebody to go to bed with— that's all you want now! What's the matter? Is your precious girlfriend frigid?'

'Leave Janice out of this,' he ordered, and she tossed him a snide look, her nose wrinkling. Glaring at her, he said, 'You seem to be forgetting a few facts, lady.

did ask you to marry me—we were engaged and *you* broke it off.'

'And weren't you relieved? It must have felt good to get that shotgun out of your back!'

'There was no shotgun,' he told her. She afforded him a look of disbelief. 'I was perfectly willing to marry you—with or without your being pregnant.'

'Oh, don't lie to me, Harris!' Her lip curled derisively. 'Next you'll be telling me you were in love with me!'

He didn't answer immediately, just looked at her with a steadfast gaze. The statement hung in the air between them, suspending time. Charlotte felt her anger ebbing, seeping away and leaving an empty shell. At last, he stated quietly, 'Obviously, you wouldn't believe me if I did.'

Her mouth felt dry and she swallowed with difficulty. He would be lying, he had to be. He had never loved her all those years ago. He had been a playboy, looking for a one-night stand. Their engagement. . .she and her father had forced him into it. It *had* been that way. When she spoke, though, it came out as a whisper. 'I couldn't believe you.'

'I didn't think you would,' he said steadily, a note of grimness deepening his voice. Charlotte found she couldn't take her eyes from him. Her stomach was knotted with tension as deep within her uncertainty churned. Harris's smoke-grey eyes never wavered from hers as he looked at her with resignation, banked with anger. He said in a soft, cold voice, 'You were the one who was always professing her love back then, weren't you?' Charlotte flinched at his reminder of her naïveté.

She'd made a fool of herself, begging him to love her back. His mouth was twisted in derision. 'But *you* were the one who got rid of our baby—handed back the ring. I would never have let you go otherwise.'

He turned and walked to the exit. Stunned, Charlotte watched him go, feeling as though he'd physically assaulted her. It had been a miscarriage, an act of God. His eyes had condemned her as a murderess, though. As he reached the door, she called out to him, 'Harris?' He didn't pause or look back, but pushed the door open and went through it.

# CHAPTER TEN

LIFE had a way of rolling on, even when one was bitterly unhappy. The hot, dry Colorado summer progressed, June giving way to July, the dog-days of August approaching. The farmers worried about running out of irrigation water, and there was talk of a return to the dust-bowl of the thirties in the eastern counties. A steady stream of cars wound its way from the plains and foothills up into the cool thin air of the Rockies, disgorging their occupants to ooh and aah over the spectacular views of craggy peaks and glacial valleys. The tourist season was one of the best on record, and Foothills had few vacancies.

Towards the end of July, Charlotte got out the books and sample lesson plans she'd collected throughout her training years and began preparing for the class she would teach in the autumn. She'd worked very hard to become a qualified teacher, studying for exams, writing papers, and all the while working at any job she could find to make a living.

Yet, as she surveyed the jumble of books and papers lying about her bedroom, she experienced a peculiar emptiness. She'd dreamed of becoming a teacher ever since childhood, but now that the dream was becoming a reality it had fallen flat.

All because of a man, she thought with self-disgust. She hadn't seen or spoken to Harris since that night

they'd argued weeks earlier and his absence in her life
had rendered it barren and joyless. He was still living
at the hotel, but, as he'd pointed out at the beginning—
it was a big place, and they could avoid each other.

And he was certainly avoiding her, she thought
desolately. She'd wasted countless hours these past few
weeks steeped in useless regret for that last meeting.
He'd said he could explain about his engagement to
Janice. She couldn't imagine what plausible explanation he could tender, but shouldn't she at least have
given him a chance?

Sighing faintly, Charlotte went on with her task of
sorting. On the other hand, it probably *was* better that
she hadn't listened to him. She just might have weak-
ened, allowed herself to be swayed by lies and false
promises. More than one of her friends had been taken
in by a married man, left waiting in limbo for him to
leave his wife and seek a divorce. The time was never
right, though, and in the end the girl eventually realised
it never would be. Harris wasn't married—yet—but
the situation was all too analogous.

She had just finished going through a stack of old
test papers when she heard a crash in the kitchen. For
one brief instant she sat motionless, then the papers
tumbled from her lap as she jumped to her feet and
rushed from the bedroom.

She found Jimmy lying on the floor of the kitchen in
a crumpled heap. Wasting no time, she knelt beside
the old man. He was conscious, but his face was
contorted with pain. 'What happened?'

'I was just getting a pack of cigarettes,' he muttered.
He tried to sit up, but quickly subsided as another

wave of pain washed over him. Sweat beaded his forehead.

Charlotte took his hand and squeezed it encouragingly, then glanced over to the overturned step-stool in front of the stove. Before she'd started storing his cigarettes in the cupboard by the sink where they were within reach, she'd kept them in one over the range. Why hadn't he remembered she'd moved them? One of her reasons for rearranging the cupboards had been so that he wouldn't need to climb up on the stool to reach things.

She looked back at her old friend. His lined face was paper-white, his pale blue eyes wide with pain. She could hear his breath coming in short, laboured spurts. 'I'm going to call an ambulance.'

She tried to disengage her hand from his in order to rise, but he held on to it with surprising strength. 'Don't do that. It'll cost a fortune. Just let me get my breath and I'll be OK,' he whispered. He managed a weak smile. 'Can't stand them damn hospitals anyway.'

Dismayed, Charlotte pursed her lips. Jimmy would be arguing with the pallbearers at his funeral! She felt a sudden stab of grief as the thought crossed her mind. It wasn't a joke, but touched too close to reality. Jimmy was eighty-five years old and at that age even a minor fall could be serious.

Feeling close to tears, she forced herself to be firm. 'I've got to. You need to be checked out. I know you've probably just picked up a couple of bruises, but *I* want to know that it's nothing more.' It was amazing what conviction one could put in one's tone when one was desperate. Old bones were terribly brittle and her elderly friend could easily have broken one. As she managed to get her hand back and went to the phone, a deeper fear nagged at her. What had caused him to fall in the first place?

Charlotte came out of the air-conditioned office building where Jimmy's doctor had his rooms into the furnace-like heat of the Colorado summer. The sun beat down on the pavement, hot enough to fry the proverbial egg, its glare painful to the eyes. None the less, Charlotte felt chilled to the bone.

Her car was parked half a block away and when she reached it she hesitated. She'd planned to visit Jimmy at the hospital this afternoon after her appointment with his doctor. For once, she was thankful for his senility. Yesterday, he hadn't comprehended her visit. If she skipped today, perhaps he wouldn't notice. She didn't think she could face him just now.

Gnawing her lower lip, she glanced at the meter. There were only a few minutes left on it, but if she put in more money she could take a walk. Opening her handbag, she rummaged inside it for change. However, when her fingers encountered the packet of materials the doctor had given her, they started to shake and she couldn't retrieve the coins.

Abruptly, she closed the bag and walked on down the street. It was a quiet neighbourhood, mainly office buildings, interspersed with older residences, and there were few pedestrians. At one house, a young man, stripped to the waist, was mowing the front lawn. He watched her approach, flexing his muscles as she neared to show off his perfect bronze tan. She didn't even glance at him.

She didn't glance at anything, or consider what she was doing or where she was going. She merely placed one foot automatically in front of the other and tried to keep her mind blank. She didn't notice the gradual change in the neighbourhood, the houses and offices giving way to shops and cafés, the pavement filling with people.

It wasn't until she jostled into one, a heavy-set woman with a sour face, that she started to snap out of it. Muttering an apology to the shopper, she moved to the inside edge of the pavement and stared into a shop window. She couldn't spend the rest of her life walking around like a zombie. She had to make some plans, some decisions, whether she liked it or not.

The shop window held a selection of goods, but her eyes were drawn to a frilly pink baby dress displayed in one corner. She should buy it for Brandy, Tony and Ann's new daughter. She'd only seen her once, at the hospital, and she should make an effort to visit Ann at home and see how she was doing.

As Charlotte stared at the dress, a dreamy confection of lace and pink bows, a hard, painful lump began to form in her throat. She'd never bought anything for her own baby—she'd lost it before she could even think of things like clothes and bedding and bottles. Nevertheless, she'd wanted it, her baby, hers and Harris's.

His parting remark still tormented her. It was obvious that he thought she'd had an abortion. She hadn't, though. One morning, she'd woken with cramps and found she was bleeding. By noon, the baby was gone. The doctor had told her it was just one of those things.

It had happened so quickly, so unexpectedly, that perhaps Harris could be forgiven for thinking she might have arranged it. There had been so little communication between them following her miscarriage—only the note she'd sent him with her ring. All these years later, she couldn't even remember how she'd worded it.

She probably hadn't explained things very well. She'd been terribly upset and somehow explaining what had happened to Harris hadn't seemed very important at the time. It had been enough for him to know the baby was gone, the wedding off. Now, though, she wished she had taken more care. She didn't want Harris thinking that of her.

She wasn't even aware that she was crying until a sob tightened her chest. She tried to blink the tears away, to control the terrible grief that was washing over her, but it was as if a floodgate had opened. The strain and unhappiness since her rift with Harris, the tension and pain since Jimmy had gone to the hospital ten days ago: her nerves were shot, her self-control overtaxed.

Wrapping her arms around her waist, she kept her back to the pavement, her head bowed so the tears fell like raindrops to the scorching pavement. A tremor shook her. She knew she was making a fool of herself, that this public display of anguish was only going to cause her embarrassment—but she couldn't seem to stem it.

She was helpless as well when a muscular arm was placed around her waist and she was pressed against a solid chest. A familiar male scent wrapped around her, a heartbeat comforting in her ear, but even Harris's secure embrace couldn't stem the flow of tears.

Charlotte swallowed hard, choking on them and trembling uncontrollably. 'That's enough now,' Harris murmured, his voice firm but soothing. None the less, fresh sobs shook her, and finally he eased her along the pavement until they reached the doorway of a vacant store. Inside the alcove, he shielded her from the view of passers-by, stroking her head and back in an age-old gesture of comfort.

She struggled to regain her equilibrium, with small success. Hiccuping, she managed to speak. 'I feel such a fool. . .having a crying jag right out here on the street.' She buried her face in the crisp cotton of his shirt as another flood of tears spurted from her eyes.

'It's OK, don't worry about it,' he reassured her. Keeping one arm firmly around her, he fumbled in his pocket for a handkerchief. Withdrawing a patterned square, he tilted her chin up and dabbed at her damp cheeks. Fully conscious that her eyes were swollen and red, still trickling tears, she tried to hide her face from him, but he wouldn't allow it.

She submitted in the end, finding the small struggle was what she had needed to regrip the reins of her self-control. Hot and damp with emotion and embarrassment, she avoided his eyes, bowing her head as his hand dropped away. He reached up, sliding his hand beneath the moist tangle of her blonde hair against the nape of her neck and gently massaging the tense muscles. It was an infinitely comforting action, but in her humiliation she couldn't respond to it.

'What happened, Charlotte?' he asked softly. She moved her shoulders dismissively, unable to answer. She didn't really know why she had broken down like that. It was true that many things were dragging her down, but over the years she'd learned self-sufficiency and discipline. She was no clinging vine or weeping willow. She faced adversity with courage. Yet even now, after that purge of emotion, she still felt the tears of heartache close at hand.

At her refusal to reply, he said, 'I've a confession to make. . .I've been watching you. I was driving by when I saw you come out of the doctor's office.'

She had to look at him, her misty lilac eyes cautious. His face was grim, his mouth controlled and his complexion tinged with grey. 'Something about the way you looked. . .' He shrugged. 'I parked and followed you.' His hands slid from her shoulders and gripped hers with painful insistence. 'I know you haven't been into work for a couple of weeks. . .I thought you were getting ready for your teaching job this fall. I wondered if maybe you'd decided to quit the Black Stallion early. That's not it, though, is it?' His eyes bored into hers. 'Can't you tell me what's wrong? Is it. . .are you ill?' he asked intently.

She shook her head, her eyes widening as she took in the urgency of his questioning, the easing of tension in his expression at her denial. He seemed. . .so worried. 'It's not me,' she told him. 'I. . .er. . .it's Jimmy.' Just saying her old friend's name brought the tears welling up to the surface again and she bit her lip to hold them back.

His mouth had firmed in reaction to the reference to the old man, but when he saw the threat to her composure he slipped his arm back around her protectively. Taking control, he moved her out on to the pavement. 'Let's go have some coffee and you can tell me about it,' he suggested bracingly.

Her head swung in refusal. 'I can't go in anywhere looking like this.' She reached up and wiped an errant tear from her cheek with the heel of her hand.

'How about my place, then?' Harris compromised. Charlotte tensed—the thought of strangers witnessing her ravaged emotions was bad enough, but to go somewhere where she was known. . . What if Janice was there?'

'I. . .'

As though reading her thoughts, he didn't force her to finish the denial. 'We'll just go for a drive,' he said quietly.

They walked back the way she had come. She felt a vague sense of unreality as Harris moved in step with her, his arm firm and secure across her back. Her spirits were lightening, as though she had moved the terrible tension and depression that had overwhelmed her earlier on to his broad shoulders. She had no reason or right to expect that he would bear her burdens, and yet she felt a sense of relief and optimism in his presence.

When they reached the block where the doctor's office was, Harris steered her towards his big white car. Charlotte lagged back. He paused, half turning to look back at her. 'My car's parked over there.' She gestured to it. 'It's on a meter and I can't leave it there any longer.' Already she could see a paper fluttering under one of the wiper blades. She must have got a parking ticket already. Next someone would tow it away.

Harris looked over to the car, frowning. After a minute or two, Charlotte took a couple of steps towards it. She was loath to leave him, but it was probably for the best. Harris was Janice's fiancé, not hers, and it wasn't right for her to depend on him. She would have to deal with her problems on her own.

However, before she could leave, he said abruptly, 'Give me your keys. We'll stop by the hotel and get someone to pick it up for you.' He held out his hand. 'You can leave it in the car park there for as long as you want.'

Charlotte stared down at the hand he held out to her. It was a powerful hand, with long fingers and clean, blunt-cut nails. There was strength and dependability in the hand, but with the capacity for gentleness, just as there was in the man.

She had a hundred reasons for not giving him the keys—the gossip that would ensue at the hotel when he asked for her car to be moved, his fiancée, her own sense of independence. And yet, she reached into her bag and handed them to him.

'The doctor says I haven't any alternative. If it was only a case of his broken hip, I might be able to manage him at home, but it's more than that. He had a minor stroke that caused him to fall in the first place and he's had a couple more since he's been in the hospital. He needs care twenty-four hours a day, and the doctor doesn't think I can cope with him.'

Charlotte paused to get a firm grip on the tears that were threatening, glancing over to Harris. He'd been terribly patient with her today. After stopping at the hotel to drop off her car keys, they'd gone for a long drive. Realising that she was still too close to the edge of despair to talk about her problems yet, he'd kept the conversation to inconsequentials. It was only now, in the seclusion of her apartment after a meal they prepared together, that he'd drawn her out of what was bothering her.

'I feel so guilty about it. He's going to hate it in one of those places.' She gestured towards the brochures of nursing homes the doctor had given that were spread out on the table between them. Harris picked one up and leafed through it.

'I think the doctor's probably right—you couldn't cope with him. These places don't look all that bad,' he opined, spreading open the pages of one pamphlet to show her an idyllic scene of flowers and clipped lawns. Two incredibly healthy-looking senior citizens were strolling along a path, laughing together. 'In fact, most of them look quite comfortable.'

'Well, would *you* like to be stuck in one?' she demanded, feeling annoyed with him. The doctor had told her much the same and she'd been annoyed with *him* too. She didn't know what she'd expected the men to do, but maybe it was to wave a magic wand and make this whole awful dilemma go away.

Harris grimaced wryly, ignoring her ill-temper. 'I don't suppose I would, but then I'm not your friend's age and I have control of all my faculties. Someday, though, who knows?' He shrugged and she gave him a sour look. He returned it with a firm one. 'Charlotte, you're going to have to face facts. From what you've told me, your friend Jimmy just isn't capable of living at home any more. Aside from his health, he's growing terribly senile. Chances are he won't even realise he's in a nursing home.'

'He isn't that bad,' she said mutinously.

'Isn't he?' Harris responded persistently. 'Didn't you tell me that yesterday when you went to see him he didn't recognise you?'

Charlotte moved her shoulders defensively. 'It was just being in the hospital—it's kind of disorientated him.' The damn tears were seeping up again and she turned her head to avoid his gaze. Why did Harris have to be so logical and so right? Jimmy probably *wouldn't* realise she'd consigned him to a nursing home—he just couldn't seem to get a grip on the present since his accident. Maybe it was the strokes he'd suffered, maybe just a progression of his disease. But she still felt guilty about what she was planning for the old man.

Harris watched the changing expressions on her face for a moment, then got up from his chair and moved around to hers. Lifting her to her feet, he cradled her in his embrace for a moment. Gently, he said, 'I know this is very hard for you, but you have to go ahead with it.'

'I know,' she admitted in a muffled voice.

'I'll help you,' he assured her. 'Tomorrow we'll go out and look at some of these places. I'll be with you every minute and we'll find somewhere that Jimmy will be happy in.'

'You think we can?' She lifted her face to peer up into his; her amethyst eyes dew-drenched violets.

'I promise.' He lowered his head to briefly touch his lips to hers, then dropped his arms from around her. 'Go on and sit in the living-room and I'll make us some coffee.'

When he came in with it a few minutes later, Charlotte was seated on the sofa, her head thrown back, her eyes closed as she listened to the record playing on the stereo. It was an old Glenn Miller album, a collector's edition. As he set the tray of coffee down, Charlotte roused herself, opening her eyes to look at him. They were dark with memories and so unbearably sad that he knew the album must belong to the old man.

He reached out his hand to hers and pulled her to his feet. 'Dance with me,' he ordered softly, pulling her into his arms. To the strains of 'String of Pearls' they slowly circled the room. Charlotte linked her arms around his waist and nestled against his shoulder, the sound of his heart in her ear. Gradually, the unhappy thoughts ebbed away and she gave herself to the exquisite joy of being held by him.

The coffee gradually cooled, and when the album ended Harris went over and found another, and after that another. It was dark outside when finally they let the silence fill the room. Still holding her in his embrace, Harris looked down into her eyes, luminous and dreamy in the soft lamplight of the room.

'I'd better go,' he said reluctantly. His mouth brushed her forehead.

As he loosened his arms to release her, hers automatically tightened. 'Er. . .we never had that coffee,' she reminded him. She couldn't bear him to leave. With him here she felt safe and secure, if not happy. As soon as he was gone, the emptiness of the apartment would close around her, the memories and loneliness rush in on her.

She knew it wasn't right to want him. He belonged to someone else. But she loved him with all her heart and needed him so badly. Tomorrow, she might feel guilt and regret, but tonight. . .

He'd glanced to where their untouched cups of coffee had grown cold. 'Are you sure you want any? It might keep you awake.' He touched the faint blue shadows that marred the delicate skin beneath her eyes. 'You've had a rough time and look as if you could use a good night's sleep.'

For a brief moment, she stared up at him, then abruptly stepped back and away. The genuine concern in his voice struck a chord of guilt within her. She'd been about to do it again. Once before, she'd needed him desperately, had thrown away her scruples for a night in his arms.

And tonight, she didn't know whether she wanted him to make love to her, or simply that she just needed the comfort of his presence, his companionship. However, if his fiancée came to hear that he'd spent the night here, no matter how innocently, it could very well wreck the relationship. What had he said when they'd first met this summer—that she'd played havoc with his life all those years ago? Did she love him so little that she could risk doing it again?

Besides, if she coaxed him to have the coffee, dance a little more, it might not be that innocent. There was no denying the sexual electricity that flashed between them, like lightning forking across a stormy sky. The temptation would be there.

'I expect you're right,' she said stiffly. 'Maybe you should be going.' She reached down and picked up a throw pillow from the sofa. Cradling it against her, she smoothed the wrinkles from it as though it were the most important task in the world. She looked at him.

He studied her thoughtfully for a moment. There was something terribly vulnerable about her. 'You sure you'll be all right here on your own? I can stay if you want me to.' She gave him a quick, sharp look and he grinned mockingly. 'I meant on the couch.'

'I——' she started uncertainly.

'Look,' he interrupted, coming to a decision, 'why don't you just go get ready for bed? I'll straighten up in here, then crash out on the couch.'

Before she quite knew what was happening, he'd hustled her off to her bedroom and the door was closed between them. For a moment, Charlotte stood leaning against it, pondering over what had just happened. At last, with a bewildered sigh, she went to find her nightie. Maybe he couldn't see the danger. Maybe, for him, there wasn't any. Whatever, it was out of her hands.

# CHAPTER ELEVEN

It was those dark hours before dawn that were often the hardest to get through. When Charlotte slid into bed, she fell quickly into a deep, dreamless sleep. However, around one-thirty, she awoke. For a long time, she lay staring up at the dark ceiling, her thoughts scurrying around like demented mice until finally she couldn't stand lying there any longer.

Quietly, she crept out of the bed and buttoned a thin cotton négligé over her light summer nightie. She had to pass through the living-room to reach the kitchen, and she eased the door open carefully. In the shadowed room, she could see Harris's dark shape stretched out on the sofa, his quiet breathing the only sound in the room. Tiptoeing to the kitchen door, she slipped through it, not turning on the light until it was closed firmly behind her.

There was instant chocolate in the cupboard, so she went to get it, although a hot drink didn't really appeal on such a warm night. However, in the cupboard behind the chocolate box she found a bottle of rum that had been there since last Christmas when she'd made fruit cake. As a rule, she didn't drink much. In her line of work, she'd seen enough alcohol abuse to be cautious of the substance. But the liquor might make her sleepy.

She was standing at the counter sipping on a mixture

of rum and cola when Harris came in a few minutes later. She glanced around at the sound of his entrance. Her heart gave a hard knock when she saw him and she quickly turned away. He'd pulled on his trousers, but he was bare-chested, his hair tousled, his face flushed with sleep. He looked unbearably dear.

'Couldn't you sleep?' he asked, and she could hear the yawn in his voice.

'Not really.' She took a quick gulp of her drink. He'd come to stand directly behind her and she was achingly conscious of his nearness. 'I'm sorry if I woke you.'

'No matter,' he dismissed. 'Having a drink?' he asked, and she knew he'd spotted the rum bottle still sitting on the counter. She felt embarrassed, although she hardly made a habit of drinking alone in the wee small hours of the morning.

'I thought it might help me get back to sleep,' she explained defensively.

'Could do.' He reached around and picked up her glass to sample it. Her eyes moved to his face and she saw his grimace. 'It would probably work a little better if you put more booze in it,' he advised, returning the glass to the counter. 'That tastes like straight Coke.'

Charlotte didn't answer, but looked at the glass. It was silly to want to touch her lips to the spot his had been, as though they could share a kiss that way.

Harris moved closer and slid his arms around her waist. He rested his chin on her shoulder and asked, 'So what woke you up? Are you still worried about Jimmy?'

'Sort of,' she hedged. Her thoughts had been all over the place, but most of them had centred on Harris himself. With his arms around her like this, the intimate atmosphere of the pre-dawn hours, she suddenly felt as though she could tell him some of those thoughts. Besides, she didn't have to face him when they were standing like this.

'Harris——' she began, then stopped to moisten her dry lips as she found it took more courage than she'd thought. 'Harris, about our baby. . .' She felt him tense fractionally and hurried on. 'I never. . .I never had an abortion.'

His arms dropped from around her and he walked a few paces away. She turned to look at him. He was standing half turned from her, his head bowed as he ran his hand over the back of his neck. Sensing her watching him, he looked over at her, his expression controlled. 'It doesn't really matter after all these years. I. . .I think I can understand. You were awfully young, Charlotte. Too young really to cope with the mess you found yourself in, and I'm not holding it against you. I'll admit I did back then, but you don't need to be ashamed of it now. I'm sure you felt that was the only way out.'

Charlotte stared at him, her eyes wide with dismay— he didn't believe her. Seeing her distress, he closed the distance between them and started to put his arms around her. She evaded him though, moving back a few feet from him. 'But I didn't get rid of the baby deliberately! It was a miscarriage—an accident of nature. I *wanted* my baby. I would never have. . .I don't know how you think that I could have!'

'Your father told me that was what you were going to do.'

'My father?' Charlotte peered at him intently. His face was horribly grim, his grey eyes dark with remembered pain. 'But my father. . .how would he. . .why would he. . .?' She just didn't understand.

'You know the business deal he wanted me to back him on?' She nodded. 'Well, when I turned him down, he threatened me. He said he wouldn't let you marry me. . .that he would make you get rid of the baby.' He stopped on seeing her stricken look, moving to take her in his arms. 'I thought he was bluffing. . .and then I got your note.'

Briefly, Charlotte rested her head against his shoulder, feeling the smooth warmth of his skin against her forehead. Then she tipped her head back to look up at him, blinking away the moisture that filmed her gaze. 'Why would he say something like that?' she asked. 'He knew he could never make me do something like that. Besides, it was such an empty threat. You didn't want to marry me in the first place.'

'Didn't I?' he asked quietly.

For a long moment, his eyes held hers, tender and soft with regret. 'You did?' she whispered, and he nodded.

'I was madly in love with you.'

Charlotte frowned and would have moved away from him, but his arms held her firmly against him. 'But you couldn't have been,' she charged, stung by his lie. 'You never acted like it! You seemed to despise me.'

His mouth twisted with chagrin. 'I know.' He sighed ruefully. 'I was a lot younger then too, don't forget. I—I resented the way I felt about you. You scared the hell out of me. I was nowhere near ready to settle down, tie myself to one woman for the rest of my life. . .and then you came along.' He reached up his hand to smooth an errant tendril of silken blonde hair from her temple.

'You bowled me over that week of the stock show. At first, I thought we could just have an affair. . .that you were just another girl and as soon as I'd taken you to bed you'd be out of my system.'

'And isn't that what happened?' she asked, the remembered pain of those weeks after the show honing a bitter edge on her voice.

He shook his head, his arms tightening about her. 'Not at all. You were right under my skin, but don't you see? I was fighting it, trying to deny it. Remember how you used to call me up?' he asked. 'I lived for those phone calls, but they were torture too. I wanted to go to you so badly, to see you, to make love to you again. But I loved my freedom, and you were a big threat to it. I loved you, but I resented you too. That's why I was so cold to you, why I wouldn't let myself go see you. I was punishing you, but I was hurting myself even more.'

Charlotte was silent, struggling to take in what he had said. It took a radical readjustment in thinking. All these years she'd thought he'd been indifferent to her, had despised her for forcing him into the engagement. 'You seemed so angry when you found out about the baby. . .that you were going to have to marry me.'

'I think at that point it was more my pride that was hurting than anything else. I was just coming around to admitting to myself that I loved you and wasn't going to be able to live without you, when suddenly I hadn't a choice. I was immature enough to resent that.' He paused a minute, thoughtful. 'I suppose what bothered me even more was that *you* weren't given a choice either. I wanted you to love me for myself, not because I was the solution to your problem.'

'But I did love you. You knew that,' she protested.

'You were only seventeen,' Harris reminded her. 'You *said* you loved me, but it could very well have been simple infatuation. You have to admit, you weren't very enthusiastic about our engagement.'

'Only because I felt guilty that I'd forced you into it.'

'It didn't take much force,' he admitted drily. 'Your father knew how I felt about you. He tried to use it to his advantage.'

Charlotte hung her head, ashamed of her father's scheming. 'He was lying to you. I would never have let him force me into something like that. . .' She trailed off. Despite the rift between them, she was none the less appalled that her own father could have been so iniquitous.

Harris gathered her closer, slipping his hand beneath the fall of her hair to stroke the tender skin at the back of her neck before tipping her face up to his. 'You aren't responsible for him. He used you more than he tried to use me.' She could feel the tension of anger in his hold, directed at the man who had almost been his father-in-law. 'When I think of what he made me believe about you. . .I'd never have let you go so easily. Can you ever forgive me for believing him?'

'Of course, darling,' she assured him, standing on tiptoe to brush her lips over his. He dropped his head to meet her kiss, his mouth warm and reassuring. Her hands slid up his ribcage to rest against his chest. Beneath her palms, his heart beat strong and steady, a rhythm in tune with hers. Her fingers tangled in the crisp curls that sprinkled his chest, then sought the hard nub of his male nipple. As her fingertips brushed over it, she felt him shudder, and his kiss deepened.

She met the demand of his growing hunger, her lips parting to give access to his tongue. He probed deep within the soft, moist cavern of her mouth, teasing her tongue, gliding over the smooth enamel of her teeth.

When his mouth slid from hers, he traced the line of her throat with his lips. With one hand, he pushed aside the frail material of her robe, and brushed fiery kisses along her collarbone. Her nightie was a barrier to his savouring touch and he pulled down the neckline. Cupping the firm swell of her breast, he drew it upwards and took the delicate blossom of her nipple into his mouth.

Charlotte's fingers dug into the hard flesh of his shoulder as a dart of ecstasy speared through her. His tongue flicked over the swollen tip of her nipple, his lips encircling the rosy swell.

'I want you so much,' he whispered against the rounded orb of her bosom, his breath warm and feather-light against her sensitive skin. He lifted his head and looked long and deep into her eyes. Pulling up her gown to her waist, he covered her buttocks with his palms and pulled her against the hard manliness of his thighs. She could feel him pressed against her lower belly, igniting a primitive hunger in her loins that threatened to consume her.

She arched towards him, allowing the ardent passion

to flow through her. His hand sought the moist, secret cave of her femininity and she shuddered with the intensity of her emotions as his fingers discovered the entrance.

'Let me love you, Charlotte,' he murmured in her ear, his tongue outlining its shell-like curve.

'Oh, yes, please,' she breathed. Silently, she begged him, 'Love me again as you did before.'

He scooped her into his arms and carried her from the kitchen to her bedroom. Gently laying her on the bed, he stood looking down at her for a moment, his silvery grey eyes bright with desire. Then he unhooked the waistband of his trousers and pushed them down over his hips, following them with his shorts.

Her eyes consumed him, the perfection of his maleness, the long, lean solidity of his body. He was broad and well-muscled, incredibly virile. Her heart accelerated as he stepped up to the bed, her breathing ragged with desire.

He looked down at her and smiled crookedly. 'You've got too many clothes on.' He reached down and pulled her to her feet, then went to work on the buttons of her robe. She watched his downbent head as he fumbled them through the holes, smiling to herself. Her fingers itched to lose themselves in the thick tangle of his hair, to cradle his dear head against her bosom.

'Damn,' he muttered.

'What's wrong?' she asked.

'This button is all screwed up.' He looked up to her, his mouth wry. 'I don't suppose you'd let me just tear this thing off you?' he asked, half serious.

Exciting as that sounded, she said, 'I don't suppose I would.' Pushing his hands away, she inspected the button. The hole had frayed slightly, and some of the threads were caught around the button, preventing it from sliding through. As she dealt with it, Harris flopped down on the bed to wait for her.

When she'd freed the button, she turned around to look at him. He was lying sprawled on the bed, one leg cocked so that his foot rested on the mattress. 'Hurry up, woman.' He grinned at her, patting the space beside him. 'Get that thing off and take care of your man.'

She gazed at him for a moment. Desire still tingled through her veins, but the small distraction of the recalcitrant button had dampened it. Her mind was no longer fogged with the mists of passion and was working all too clearly.

She drew the robe more closely about her. 'I don't think we should, Harris,' she said quietly. The smile faded from his face and he looked at her intently.

'Why not?' he asked.

She tried to make light of it, although it was painful. 'Well, you really aren't *my* man, are you? You belong to Janice—you're engaged to her.'

For a moment, he didn't reply. Then he said, 'And that bothers you?'

'Of course it does—it should bother *you* too, Harris,' she reminded him. She couldn't help being terribly disappointed in him. Oh, she loved him and wanted him, but she also wanted to respect him. She didn't respect infidelity.

When it looked as if he had nothing more to say to

her, she turned to go back to the kitchen. Despite everything, the urge to join him on that bed was still overwhelming, and she didn't trust herself to stay. Before she reached the door, though, he called out to her, 'What if I told you that I'm not marrying Janice?'

She hesitated, but didn't trust herself to look back at him. 'Is that true?'

He got up from the bed and crossed over to her. Gently, he placed his hands on her shoulders and turned her to face him. He looked down into her wide, violet eyes with intensity. 'I'm not marrying her,' he said firmly, his gaze never wavering.

For a moment, Charlotte hovered on the brink of indecision. He looked so sincere, yet why hadn't he told her before that he'd broken his engagement? But then, they hadn't seen each other for weeks until today. She hadn't been into work lately either, so she wasn't up to date on the gossip circling the hotel.

'You're not marrying her?' she asked huskily.

He shook his head, then lowered it to kiss her. Her mouth was soft and pliant beneath his as she responded without reservation. That last terrible barrier between them had crumpled to ashes and her love flowed out to him. When he put an arm about her shoulders to lead her back to the bed, she went with him eagerly, her heart overflowing with joy.

'So what do you think of it?' Harris asked her. They were sitting in his car parked before an imposing building of wood and glass, surrounded by verdant green lawns. Giving her time to answer, he didn't start the ignition but let his hands rest lightly on the steering-wheel.

'It seems very nice,' Charlotte said dully.

He gave her a vexed look. 'Don't overwhelm me with your enthusiasm,' he replied drily, then half turned in his seat to face her. Subduing his impatience, he spoke coaxingly. 'Look, I thought you'd come to accept that this was the only solution for Jimmy. You know you can't bring him home, and this place. . .' he gestured to the building '. . .is far and away the best we've looked at so far.'

Charlotte sighed, averting her guilty eyes from him by looking out of the window. Harris was right—the Columbine Nursing Facility *was* far and away the best place they'd toured—and they'd seen a lot of places over the past three days. Some had been ghastly: dark, gloomy warehouses filled with apathetic old people waiting to die. Others had been clinically bright and antiseptically clean, with all the warmth and homeyness of a military basic training camp.

The Columbine was neither of those. Clean and modern, it somehow escaped being hospital-like. The rooms, although fitted with hospital beds, were cheerful and much like the bedrooms in private homes. The community-rooms had a 'community' spirit about them and the staff seemed warm and caring. There was, in fact, only one flaw.

Aware that Harris was still watching her, expecting some response, Charlotte hovered in indecision. He'd been so good to her these past few days, traipsing all over the country with her to find a home for Jimmy and neglecting his work at the hotel.

They shared an intimate relationship. Although he hadn't actually moved in with her, he'd only gone back to his apartment at the hotel to change clothes. They were spending their nights and days together, growing closer, developing a sound relationship.

None the less, Charlotte was still reluctant to broach the subject of money with him. The truth of the matter was that, although the Columbine was nearly perfect for Jimmy, it was also very expensive. Even with the government assistance the old man was entitled to, she would have a hard time making up the shortfall out of her teaching salary.

The solution would be to keep her job at the Black Stallion as well. And she was going to have to find out if that would be possible before she could commit herself.

Looking over at her companion, she said, 'I'm sorry I've been dithering. I do like this place and think Jimmy will too. The only thing is. . .' She paused to take a deep breath then continued quickly, 'Can I keep my job?'

Harris frowned in puzzlement. 'Your job? But I have no say over your teaching job. I— —'

'I don't mean that job,' she interrupted. 'I mean my job at the Black Stallion.' Harris's frown was starting to turn into a scowl and she rushed on, 'Look, this place isn't cheap. I'm going to need some extra income to swing it. If I could hang on to my waitressing job, even if only for the weekends, it could make all the difference.'

He treated her to an impatient look. 'You can't do two jobs.'

'That's more or less what I've been doing for the past five years,' she argued. 'It's not that big a deal, and I need to get the money from somewhere.'

He took a moment's thought before responding, then suggested, 'I don't suppose it occurred to you that you could ask me for it?' He was smiling at her now. 'I don't know how much you need, but I don't think it'll break me.'

She'd been afraid he might suggest that. It was why she hadn't wanted to bring the subject up in the first place. She couldn't take his money. She had her pride, after all. They were lovers, certainly, but really, what else was she to him? If she took his money, even if it was for Jimmy, it would almost be as though he were keeping her. She couldn't accept that.

'No,' she said flatly. 'Thank you, but no. I can't take your money.'

'Why not?' he wanted to know, a faintly hurt expression clouding his grey eyes. When she didn't answer, he burst out angrily, 'You can't want to hang on to that sleazy job! Or maybe you enjoy parading around half naked in front of a bunch of ogling drunks!'

'Well, maybe that's better than what you have in mind for me,' she muttered under her breath, stung by his condemnation of her job. She'd suspected he didn't approve of it—that he looked down on her for doing it.

He'd heard her. 'And what is that supposed to mean?' he demanded.

Charlotte shifted uncomfortably in her seat, not wanting to argue with him, yet unwilling to give in. Finally, she said, 'Well, really, Harris, you should

know why I can't take your money. We. . .
just. . .don't have that kind of relationship.'

'What kind of relationship do we have, then?' he
wanted to know.

She was getting piqued. Why couldn't he just drop
it, accept her refusal and let it go? As he continued
glaring at her in offended silence, she was goaded to
answer, 'It's pretty obvious, isn't it? You haven't
exactly been wearing out the sheets in *your* apartment
lately. I haven't had an easy time over these past few
years, but I haven't stooped to being anyone's paid
mistress yet—and I don't intend to start now!'

'So that's what you think I want—to keep you as my
mistress.'

'With the accent on the "keep" part!'

His eyes bore into hers, his face dark and furious.
Charlotte shrank back into her seat, intimidated by his
anger. Abruptly, he turned away from her and reached
for the ignition key to start the car engine. Slamming
the car into reverse, he backed out of the parking space
and headed the car back into the city.

While they'd been talking, the sky had clouded over
and now huge raindrops splattered the windscreen as
they drove along. Harris reached down and switched
on the wipers. The rhythmic swish of the blades, the
hum of the tyres over the road filled the silence that
gaped between the two people.

Occasionally, Charlotte stole secret glances at
Harris's profile. His jaw was set in hard fury, his eyes
riveted on the road ahead. As the storm worsened, she
felt that the external elements were mocking the tur-
bulence of their relationship. Harris was violently

angry, but she knew he was hurt too. She shouldn't have said that to him, but he'd annoyed her. She knew he'd only offered the money out of generosity and concern for her situation. However, if she took it, she *would* feel as though it cheapened her and their relationship.

None the less, she felt an apology was in order. She didn't like being in conflict with him. 'About what I said. . .I'm sorry. I wasn't very gracious and I didn't mean all those things. I know you were just trying to help.'

He didn't look at her to acknowledge the apology, but merely grunted and shrugged his shoulders. They continued to drive in tense silence for several more minutes, until he said, 'I've got to swing by the hotel. Your car's still there. Maybe it would be a good time for you to pick it up and take it back to your place.'

Her car had been there for three days and it hadn't bothered him before now. Obviously he was still put out with her, but it might be better to leave the matter for the time being. She still needed to know if he'd let her keep her job, but she would give him a chance to cool off before pursuing the matter.

At the hotel, he drew up behind her car and stopped to let her out. He stared straight ahead as she fumbled to unfasten her belt, making no move to get out and open the door for her. Finally she was free, and, her hand on the door lever, she turned to say goodbye and thank him for helping her with the nursing homes. However, she remained silent when she took in the set look of his expression, the still angry line of his mouth

He didn't need to cool off—if he got any colder, he'd get hypothermia!

Well, let him be mad! She'd apologised—there wasn't much more she could do. Without a word, she pushed open the door and got out into the drenching rain, As soon as she'd closed it behind her, Harris put the Cadillac into motion and drove away. As it passed, the back wheels went through a puddle and sprayed the bottom of her trousers with muddy water. She shot the retreating car a filthy look, then looked down to assess the damage to her trousers.

She was swearing to herself when Harris came up to her. 'I'm sorry, Charlotte,' he said contritely, pulling a handkerchief out of his pocket and stooping down to dab at the muddy stain on the hem of her trousers. 'I didn't mean to do that.'

'Didn't you?' she asked waspishly.

He looked up at her. The rain was streaming down his face, his hair flattened to his scalp. It made him look younger and somehow vulnerable. He pulled a rueful face, 'I didn't, really, although I suppose the way I was acting I can't blame you for thinking I might do something so childish.' He stood up and took her hands in his. 'My only excuse was that I was hurt because you wouldn't let me help you.'

'I'm sorry about all those awful things I said about you. I—I shouldn't have, and I didn't mean them.'

'I know that,' he assured her. 'As for the money. . .well, let's just drop it for now. You can think it over for a while.'

Thinking it over wasn't going to change her mind,

but it was so nice to have their disagreement put behind them that she wasn't going to pursue it now.

She smiled up at him. Her face was tipped up to his, her complexion rain-washed and fresh, her sodden hair hanging in dripping rats' tails. Nevertheless, he thought she looked incredibly lovely.

He brushed a light kiss across her mouth and a brilliant flash lit up the sky. 'We're probably going to get struck by lightning,' he murmured.

She laughed, gesturing to the tempestuous heavens and the lightning forking in jagged streams. 'That happens every time you kiss me!'

'It does?' he asked delightedly, finding her lips with his once again. All too quickly, though, he broke off the kiss as thunder rumbled in the distance. 'I love doing this, but I think we'd better continue inside where it's safer.' Giving her hand a sharp tug to urge her along, they ran hand in hand together to the back entrance of the hotel.

# CHAPTER TWELVE

THEY came into the hotel, laughing and breathless. Like rolling storm-clouds, their quarrel had passed on and, regardless of the weather outside, the sun was shining for them. With Harris's arm secure about Charlotte's waist, they walked down the corridor. Doors to the employee lounge and bar exited off it, and halfway down a hallway branched off and led to the service lift. They made for this, but hadn't reached it when Tony came through the bar door.

'I'd heard you were back at the hotel and wanted to catch you, Mr Jordan,' he said eagerly, leaving Charlotte dumbfounded at the speed with which the Foothills grapevine transmitted news. No more than fifteen minutes could have elapsed since Harris had driven into the car park.

As the bartender sent her a curious glance, she felt her face flush to scarlet. Whoever had seen Harris drive in had probably witnessed those kisses in the rain as well. The whole hotel probably knew about them by now.

Harris said, 'We're soaking wet. Can't it wait?'

Tony looked slightly crestfallen, but persisted, 'It's not urgent, but I've got something I'm anxious for you to see.' He looked at Charlotte. 'You too, Charlie.'

She looked up at Harris, smoothing the wet strands of hair back from her face. It might be better if she didn't go up to Harris's apartment with him. She liked to keep her private life just that—private—and if the gossips already knew he'd kissed in the car park they'd really have something to chatter about if she went up to the penthouse with him.

'Let's see what Tony wants to show us,' she petitioned.

Harris looked down at her, frowning doubtfully, 'You're sure? You should get out of those wet clothes.'

Acutely conscious that Tony was listening to every word they exchanged, she wished he'd worded that a little differently! However, she said, 'I'm fine. I'm not cold.'

Harris didn't look too happy about it, but he said, 'OK, then, we'll have a quick look.'

The bartender beamed and led them into the Black Stallion. Once there, he made a sweeping gesture towards the back wall of the bar. The array of liquor bottles that usually fronted it had been moved. On the blank space where Annabelle had hung, a new painting had appeared.

Charlotte stared at it, her first thought, At least he didn't paint me nude. However, as she continued her study of the oil, she wondered if the scanty wisps of cloth Tony had provided her image with weren't more erotic than bare skin would have been.

She was depicted wearing a scarlet waitress costume, although in reality she didn't think that they were cut quite so low in front, nor so high in the leg. They weren't *that* tight either—moulding her body like a second skin, the curve of her waist and hips, the outline of her breasts unconcealed. She was shown standing at the bar, one foot resting on the brass foot-rail, her head tipped back as she laughed. There was sensuality in the very line of her stance, provocation in the tilt of her head. That much she saw. She didn't take in the shy vulnerability in her eyes, the innocent radiance of her smile.

'So what do you think?' the bartender demanded of his stunned audience. 'You said you wanted something with a little more pizzazz than a landscape.' Charlotte pulled her gaze from the oil to look at Harris, realising he had been as silent as herself. The shocked expression he wore had her attention going to Tony. He appeared so thoroughly pleased with himself that she just didn't have the heart to tell him what she really thought of the painting.

'It's. . .it's very nice,' she offered lamely.

'Nice!' Tony yelped, affronted by the lukewarm compliment. 'It's the best thing I've ever done!'

Harris hissed at her, 'Did you pose for that?'

'Of course not!' Charlotte whispered back harshly.

'Well, thank God for that!' He threw the painting a scathing look of pure disgust.

Charlotte slid a quick look at Tony to see whether he had heard them. Harris's tone of voice, even without that look, had been enough to tell the bartender that his boss hated the painting. She hoped her friend wasn't too hurt. However, Tony wasn't listening to them, but contemplating his handiwork with a satisfied expression on his face.

In an undertone, she said to the man beside her, 'It isn't that bad.'

'Ummph,' he grunted, slashing the painting with his

gaze. 'As if it isn't bad enough that you persist in working here. . .now I'm expected to have that thing hanging around!' He gestured angrily to the 'thing', his face a mask of ill-humour.

She'd known all along that he didn't think highly of her employment, but she hadn't realised he was such an errant snob! She wasn't ashamed of the work she'd done at the Black Stallion. It earned her an honest living and, if for a time it had required she wear a revealing costume, then at least she'd done so with dignity, she thought, glaring at Harris.

Tony left off his meditation of his accomplishment and looked at the couple. He frowned as he read the tension arcing between them. 'What's the matter?' he asked.

Harris turned on him. 'Get rid of that damn. . .*thing*,' he spluttered. 'You never had permission to hang it in here and I want it out!'

Her co-worker stepped back from the obvious fury of his employer, his face paling. Charlotte could see the hurt robbing his eyes of their brightness and felt a surge of compassion for him. Tony was an artist, and he'd worked long and hard on the portrait. She wished he hadn't used her as his model, but from a purely aesthetic point of view his work was outstanding. She turned to defend her friend, but wasn't given the opportunity.

'So here you are, Harry.' A light, feminine voice coated with acid announced Janice's arrival. She was smiling smugly as the three protagonists turned to face her. She glanced past them at the painting, her narrow, arched brows lifting as she studied it. Then she looked at Charlotte.

'That's very good,' she told her. 'I'd say it captures the "real you".' Charlotte's lips tightened at the all too obvious insult, but before she could retort Janice moved her attention to Harris. 'You've been a very elusive man these past few days,' she informed him, sliding Charlotte a meaningful look. 'As soon as I heard you were in the hotel, I figured I'd better come find you.' She reached down and pulled the emerald that adorned her finger from her hand and held it out to Harris. 'Don't you think you ought to have this back?'

In horror, Charlotte watched Harris as he stared down at the ring the woman held out to him. It was a distinctive piece of jewellery. When Janice had first arrived at the hotel wearing it, eyes had popped. Over three carats in weight, square-cut and flawlessly brilliant, the ring Harris had bestowed on his intended bride had caused envy in the hearts of nearly every girl in the hotel.

Dragging her gaze from it, Charlotte looked at the man, feeling sick with contempt and disillusionment. All this time, he'd been engaged to Janice. Three days ago—three *nights!*—she'd asked him straight out whether he was marrying the woman—and he'd lied!

As he reached out to accept the ring, he glanced at Charlotte. Her expression told him what she was thinking. Dropping his hand, he took a step towards her, saying, 'Wait a second, Charlotte.'

But she wasn't waiting for anything, particularly not more of his lies. Turning on her heel, she ran from the

lounge. As she stepped out into the hallway, it was
plunged into darkness. She heard a crash behind her
and Harris's voice swearing loudly. The storm must
have brought down some power lines, but the sudden
blackout gave her a few minutes' lead time. The exit
door was straight down the hall, and she ran for it
before the emergency generators kicked in to use and
Harris could pursue her.

Outside, the storm was a raging torrent. Wind-
whipped rain pelted her, resoaking her clothes and
nearly blowing her off her feet. Nevertheless, she
plunged into the tempest, running for her car. With
shaking fingers, she fumbled to fit the key into the
lock, starting with fright as a jagged fork of lightning
struck a nearby car. The rain was falling in sheets, the
wind blowing the trees sideways. It was a day for
staying inside, safe and warm by a log-fed fire—not
one for driving.

However, when she got the car door open, she threw
herself behind the wheel and worked the ignition. It
took a moment to fire—the car was old and had been
sitting for some days. In her rear-view mirror, she
caught sight of Harris coming out of the hotel, and it
added desperation to her attempts to start the engine.

It fired as he started running towards her. Slamming
the car's ancient gears into reverse, she spun out of the
parking space, then put the car into forward to race for
the exit.

The old vehicle stalled as she slowed to turn on to
the street. Cursing under her breath, Charlotte twisted
the key, grinding the starter motor. Rain, mixed with
leaves from the Chinese elms that flanked the entrance,

pelted the car. The sky flamed as lightning flashed, followed immediately by the crash of thunder.

Stealing a moment to check the rear-view mirror, she saw Harris running towards the stationary vehicle. In a final desperate effort, she cranked the engine and it caught just as a bolt of lightning hit the tree at the edge of the drive. It shuddered, then toppled as Charlotte engaged the gear to drive away.

The car rocked under the force of the falling elm. Its limbs shattered the windscreen, its trunk crashing the bonnet and front end. Thrown sideways during the impact, Charlotte gingerly pushed herself back into a sitting position. In shocked incredulity, she stared at the tangle of branches and leaves surrounding her. Her mind felt muzzy, her temple throbbing from the bruise it had gathered when her head had hit the far side door. Disorientated and bewildered, she stared at the long scratch on her forearm, watching the crimson beads of blood collect along the line. She might have stared at it for hours if it hadn't wavered and faded from her vision as she slid gently into unconsciousness.

Someone was trying to force something vile and foul-smelling down her throat, and Charlotte struggled to evade them. The back of her head was clasped in a firm vice-like hold, though, her arms wrapped at her side as though she wore a strait-jacket, and she had to swallow the liquid. It burned all the way down and her eyes flew open, her mouth twisted with revulsion.

'What was that?' she demanded, surprised to find her voice barely above a whisper.

'Brandy,' Harris told her gently, setting the glass

aside. He was seated beside her on a couch in his apartment. She looked up at him from the enshrouding fold of a blanket, wrapped around her so tightly that she felt like a trussed chicken.

'It tasted awful!' she declared, struggling to free herself from the restrictive folds of the wrap. His face wry—it had been the finest Napoleon brandy, after all—Harris helped her free her arms but kept the covering securely around her back and legs. 'What happened?' Charlotte asked when she was more comfortable.

'Don't you remember?' His brow furrowing with concern, he reached up to gently stroke the bruise that darkened her temple.

Her head ached and she had to force herself to concentrate. 'There was this tree. . .' Memory trickled through and she gave him a look of fury. She would have bolted from the room had that damn blanket not been tangled around her like an octopus's arms.

As it was, she still tried to struggle to her feet. Harris leaned over her, pinning her against the back of the couch with his hand on her shoulders.

'Now, simmer down, Charlotte,' he advised her. 'You've been hurt. You can't go dashing off. I've called you a doctor, but with the storm and all it'll take him a while to get here. In the meantime, just stay quiet and rest.'

'I don't need a doctor!' she spat at him, although in truth the minor skirmish had left her feeling weak and breathless. She couldn't get away from him, move from the sofa, but she could still use her voice. 'All I need is to get away from you. . .you two-timing louse!'

He gave her a long, considering look, then his lips twisted bitterly. 'I suppose I might deserve that, but if you'd just let me explain——'

'Explain all those lies you told me to get me into bed with you?' she cut him off. 'Explain how you were going to marry Janice and keep me on the side? Did it ever occur to you I might get pregnant? It *has* happened before, you know!'

Instead of looking dismayed as she had expected him to, he actually looked pleased. 'Do you think you might be?'

She gave him an exasperated look. 'I don't know. It's too early to say,' she muttered, fingering the folds of the blanket distractedly. Harris was confusing her— it wasn't fair, after all she'd been through in the accident.

'Oh.' He sounded disappointed, then went on, 'I wasn't lying to you when I said I wasn't marrying Janice.' Since words didn't seem to be getting her anywhere, she contented herself with throwing him a look of utter disbelief. He caught up her hands and, holding them firmly in his, peered intently into her eyes. 'Look, honey, if I'm going to marry anyone, it's going to be you.'

Now *that* hurt—the biggest lie of them all! She tried to pull her hands free but he wouldn't let them go. She glared at him and he smiled coaxingly. 'I mean it, darling. I love you dearly and I want you for my wife.'

'B-b-bull feathers!' she spluttered. 'You were engaged to Janice!'

'Not any more!'

'Ummph.'

'OK, look, I know I wasn't completely honest with you before, and I'm sorry.' He dropped her hands and, half turning from her, leaned over and rested his forearms on his thighs. Despite herself, Charlotte found her heart reaching out to him. He looked sad and incredibly weary, staring down at his hands as though he'd never seen them before.

When at last he spoke, it was in a slow, painful voice. 'I found myself in one hell of a mess. Janice and I had just gotten engaged when you came back into my life again. I thought I was over you and I'd reached the stage in my life when I was ready to settle down, have a family. I've known Janice for a long time and I figured we'd make a good match. I wasn't in love with her, but it really didn't seem to matter.' He looked over to her briefly. 'I'd been in love once before and it didn't work out, so I wasn't eager to try it again.' He fell silent, his fingers doing push-ups against one another.

She hadn't wanted to listen to him, but she found herself prompting him anyway. 'So you decided to marry Janice?'

'That's right. I didn't think she cared whether I loved her or not. She needed security and I felt sorry for her. I thought it would work out.'

Charlotte pursed her lips in puzzlement. 'Why would you feel sorry for her?' she asked. Personally she thought Janice was a stuck-up prig, and couldn't see her as an object of anyone's pity.

'Oh, she's had a rough life. Her father died when she was a child and her mother was something of an invalid. I think she was a hypochondriac, but she kept

Janice tied to her apron-strings by hovering at death's door for years. She never let the girl have fun, go out and meet people of her own age. Anyway, when she died last winter, Janice seemed at a loss. I know this probably sounds terribly conceited, but I thought I was doing her a favour really by asking her to marry me.'

Maybe Janice hadn't had things all that easy, Charlotte thought grudgingly. She didn't voice her concession, though, but responded to his last statement. 'And weren't you doing her a favour?'

He leaned back against the couch and looked over at her, his smile self-derisive. 'To be honest, no. She'd just gained her freedom from that tyrant of a mother—what she really needed was a chance to enjoy that freedom, not become tied down by an engagement. To make things worse, when you came back into my life I found out I wasn't happy about being tied by one either.'

'But that was at the beginning of the summer,' she reminded him. 'You've stayed engaged to her all this time.'

'I know.' He rubbed his forefinger against his temple. 'At first, I guess, I simply didn't want to admit that I still loved you. I'd been fighting against loving you for so many years that it was something of a habit. I finally admitted to myself that it was a losing battle that night Gary tried to rape you—I wanted to kill him for even looking at you. I probably would have if they hadn't pulled me off him and stopped the fight.'

Charlotte trembled. He could have been sent to prison, and it would have been on her account. 'I. . .'

She shook her head, not knowing what to say to him. To think, he would have killed for her.

She looked over at him, loving him for his passionate nature, but half fearful of it as well. Her hand moved tentatively to reach out to him, then fell to her lap. 'You didn't break off with Janice then,' she said flatly, cursing herself for nearly softening towards him. 'I heard about your quarrel with her. *She* wanted to end the engagement, but you wouldn't let her.'

'It was because of Gary Sanders.'

'Gary? What did he have to do with it?'

'She wanted to marry him instead.'

'Well, why not let her, then?' Charlotte demanded. 'You're taking a pretty dog-in-the-manger attitude if you ask me.'

'Now just hold on and let me finish the story,' he advised. 'I didn't ever love Janice, and at that point I didn't want to marry her any more. But try to understand, Charlotte, I did feel a certain responsibility towards her.' He gave her an imploring look. 'I don't have to tell you of all people what a rotter Gary is. Janice has led a very sheltered life. Granted she needed her freedom, from her mother and from me—but not to waste it on the likes of that scoundrel. I felt I had to buy her some time to come to her senses—holding her to our engagement was the only way I could think of to keep them apart.'

Charlotte considered his explanation, not looking at him but toying distractedly with the edge of the blanket.

'I've admitted to myself now that I shouldn't have continued to interfere. She's going to have to make her own mistakes from now on—and if Gary is one of them, well, then, so be it.' He moved closer, sliding his arm around her back and taking her chin into his hand to turn her face to him. 'I wanted to explain all this to you before, but you wouldn't let me. Then, well. . .I thought maybe it would be better to stay away from you until the situation had resolved itself.' His mouth touched hers, then he moved his head back to look into her wide violet eyes. 'I couldn't wait that long, though. I knew you needed me when your friend fell ill. I couldn't stay away.'

'You lied to me,' she accused him unhappily. 'I asked you about Janice and you said you'd broken it off.'

'I didn't say that exactly—I said I wasn't marrying her, and that was the truth.' She gave him a reproachful look and he admitted, 'I know you thought I meant I'd ended the engagement. It was a white lie in that sense. But can you forgive me anyway? If you recall our circumstances when we had that discussion, maybe you can understand that I didn't have the patience right then to go into a long explanation.'

His arms closed more firmly around her, and he sought her lips with his. She met him more than halfway, her mouth opening to his, drinking in the honeyed sweetness of his kiss. The blanket fell from her shoulder and he kneaded her willing flesh. There was passion in the kiss, gentle demand, but a certain restraint too.

All too soon he pulled back from her, his face slightly flushed, the ardour in his eyes dampening. 'Don't let

me forget you've been hurt.' He glanced at his watch.
'I wonder what's happened to that doctor.'

'I'm fine. I don't need a doctor.' She needed to be
back in his arms! However, he didn't co-operate.

Sitting back against the sofa, he let his arm rest
lightly across her shoulders but didn't kiss her again.
He picked up her hand and stroked it gently.
'Charlotte,' he asked after a moment, 'would you be
terribly upset if you found out you were pregnant?'

The question startled her, coming so unexpectedly.
'I. . .I don't know, I haven't really thought about it.'

'I think you should. We've been pretty careless.' He
glanced over to her. 'I want us to get married right
away, but we should probably hold back on the kids
for a while.'

'Oh. . .OK.' Did he want to see how things worked
out first? she wondered. Divorce was easy when there
weren't any children involved.

He'd watched the thoughts chasing around her face
and his arm tightened. 'I don't know what exactly
you're thinking, but I think you've read me wrong. I
want you to have my babies—tomorrow if it were
possible. But you've worked hard to earn your qualifi-
cations—I just thought maybe you'd want to spend a
few years teaching before raising a family.'

'I hadn't thought of that,' Charlotte admitted, then
smiled up at him. 'I really *would* like a chance to
pursue my career for a while after we're married.'
Squirming closer to him, she lifted her head to kiss him
but he put his hand to her mouth. She took his finger
between her teeth and nibbled it. He gave her a
chastening look and pulled his hand away.

'If you want a career then we'd better cut this stuff out until we're a little more prepared. No sense taking any more chances.'

She would have liked to argue, but knew she had to agree. 'I suppose you're right.' It would be easier to keep to that decision if he weren't sitting quite so close, but fortunately the doorbell rang just then.

'That must be the doctor,' Harris announced, and got up to answer it. However, when he returned, he brought Tony with him.

The bartender said, 'I heard you'd been in an accident. I just came up to see how you were.'

'I'm fine,' Charlotte assured him. It was true. Her head had stopped hurting some time ago—just about the time Harris had finished explaining about his engagement to Janice, in fact! She gave that man a disgruntled look. 'Harris says I have to see a doctor, though.'

'It probably wouldn't hurt,' Tony allowed. He looked awkward and a shade uncomfortable—like a little boy sent to the principal's office. 'I wanted to apologise. . .to you both. About the painting. . .I thought as long as it wasn't a nude——'

'Forget it,' Harris interrupted. 'As a matter of fact, I'd like to buy it from you.'

'You would?' both Tony and Charlotte exclaimed at once. She fell silent, but the bartender asked, 'You mean to put Annabelle back?'

Harris shook his head. 'I'd like you to do a different one for the bar—another nude.' He gave the man a stern look. 'Only this time—hire a model and don't use your friends.'

'Sure, whatever you say!' Tony was beaming.

It was Charlotte who asked, 'But what about Tony's painting of me?'

'I'll hang it up here—right over my bed.'

Before Charlotte could get her astonished tongue untangled to question Harris, Tony was taking his leave. 'I'd better get back downstairs. I just slipped up to see how Charlie was.' He stuck out his hand to the other man. 'Thanks for the commission.'

'Come see me tomorrow and we'll discuss the financial arrangements,' Harris suggested, ushering him to the door.

When he came back, Charlotte burst out, 'But you hated that painting!'

He was shaking his head, and came forward to lift her into his embrace. 'Obviously you don't understand your future husband very well. I love the painting.' His mouth brushed hers, leaving her aching for more. 'I *love* the subject! I just don't want anyone else loving her! I'm a very jealous man. It just about drove me round the bend having you work downstairs, looking incredibly beautiful and sexy in that get-up you wore.' He pulled back to grin at her. 'By the way, you're fired. I'm not going through the torture any longer of all those other men seeing you like that. . .' he kissed her eyes, her nose, the curve of her cheek '. . .and falling as madly in love with you as I am.'

'I thought you were ashamed of me, ashamed of the job I did.'

He pulled away from her abruptly, his look of utter astonishment convincing her that she had been wrong to label him a snob. 'But——'

She cuddled closer to him, raising her lips for his kiss. 'I love you madly too,' she side-tracked. She was ashamed of herself for even thinking Harris could be so bigoted. The less said now, the better. 'Don't you think we've talked long enough?' she pouted.

'But——'

'Oh, just kiss me, darling.'

He gave her a wry look. 'Just because you no longer work for me, don't expect we'll turn things around and let you be *my* boss.' However, he kissed her thoroughly—and with relish—none the less!

## THIS JULY, HARLEQUIN OFFERS YOU
## THE PERFECT SUMMER READ!

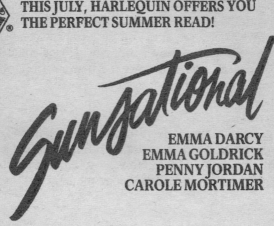

### EMMA DARCY
### EMMA GOLDRICK
### PENNY JORDAN
### CAROLE MORTIMER

From top authors of Harlequin Presents comes
HARLEQUIN SUNSATIONAL, a four-stories-in-one
book with 768 pages of romantic reading.

Written by such prolific Harlequin authors as Emma Darcy,
Emma Goldrick, Penny Jordan and Carole Mortimer,
HARLEQUIN SUNSATIONAL is the perfect summer
companion to take along to the beach, cottage, on your
dream destination or just for reading at home in the warm
sunshine!

**Don't miss this unique reading opportunity.**

Available wherever Harlequin books are sold.

SUN

# Take 4 bestselling love stories FREE
## Plus get a FREE surprise gift!